CARTEL KILLAZ

Lock Down Publications and Ca$h
Presents
Cartel Killaz
A Novel by *Hood Rich*

Lock Down Publications

P.O. Box 870494
Mesquite, Tx 75187

Visit our website @
www.lockdownpublications.com

First Edition October 2019
Printed in the United States of America

This is a work of fiction. Names, characters, places, and incidents either are products of the author's imagination or are used fictitiously. Any similarity to actual events or locales or persons, living or dead, is entirely coincidental.

Lock Down Publications
Like our page on Facebook: Lock Down Publications @
www.facebook.com/lockdownpublications.ldp
Cover design and layout by: **Dynasty Cover Me**
Book interior design by: **Shawn Walker**
Edited by: **Jill Alicea**

Stay Connected with Us!

Text **LOCKDOWN** to 22828 to stay up-to-date with new releases, sneak peaks, contests and more…

Thank you.

Submission Guideline.

Submit the first three chapters of your completed manuscript to ldpsubmissions@gmail.com, subject line: Your book's title. The manuscript must be in a .doc file and sent as an attachment. Document should be in Times New Roman, double spaced and in size 12 font. Also, provide your synopsis and full contact information. If sending multiple submissions, they must each be in a separate email.

Have a story but no way to send it electronically? You can still submit to LDP/Ca$h Presents. Send in the first three chapters, written or typed, of your completed manuscript to:

LDP: Submissions Dept
Po Box 870494
Mesquite, Tx 75187

DO NOT send original manuscript. Must be a duplicate.

Provide your synopsis and a cover letter containing your full contact information.

Thanks for considering LDP and Ca$h Presents.

Hood Rich

Chapter 1

Mudman took a strong swallow from the pink Sprite and wiped his mouth with the back of his hand. His eyes felt heavy. He struggled to keep them open. He pulled the Draco onto his lap and cocked it. "Say, mane, I'm 'bout to cause a whole lot of static, homeboy. Ma'fuckas 'bout to give me all dat shit they got in dat bitch, I'm letting you know that right now." He aimed the mini assault rifle at a random place on the wall and smiling sinisterly.

Mudman was 5'11" tall and weighed in at 220 pounds. He had gray eyes and was dark as sin. He was so dark that to most, he looked scary and evil. He had long dreadlocks that fell to the middle of his back. He kept them neatly twisted unless he was hunting a certain prey. When it came down to hunting, Mudman couldn't care less how he looked until he got his prey.

Prentice took the syringe and injected a hefty dosage of the Sinaloa Tar. He groaned and pulled the needle out, setting it on the table. Prentice was six feet even, with brown eyes and caramel skin. He weighed in at a healthy 180 pounds. Prentice had a bald head that looked as if it needed to be shaven again. Prentice was Mudman's first cousin and right hand man, for the most part. Mudman was mostly a lethal loner, but every now and then he chose to do dirt with Prentice. Both men were deadly in their own right.

"Say, mane, you ain't been home for more than two days, and already you tryna get yo' feet dirty?" Prentice asked. He felt the effects of the heroin taking over him. He closed his eyes, and then opened them again. His body felt numb. The beats of his heart slowed. The injection site where he took his heroin was itching worse than a dog that obtained a family of fleas. He scratched it until blood appeared. "Mane, this ain't the same Baton Rouge that you remember, homeboy. Dese niggas out here killing for fun. Trust me when I tell you dat shit right thurr."

Mudman shook two Percocets into his hand before popping them and scooting forward on the couch. He aimed the Draco at Prentice and curled his upper lip. "Ma'fucka, I been gone for five years. Five years I been in Angola, working dem fuckin' fields for dem people, and ain't a ma'fucka sent me a crumb. Now da way I see it, dese ma'fuckas owe me, mane. Fo' I left, I made sho' all these fake-ass dope boys was eating, and all dey asses forgot about me once them bars slammed in my face. You say Munchie 'n 'em holding what up in that club?" Mudman asked, still keeping the shotgun pinned on Prentice.

Prentice sucked his good teeth and curled his upper lip. "Nigga, you got 'bout three seconds to get dat fuckin' gun off of me, or else we finna splatter these walls with each other's blood. I don't know what you thank dis is, but ain't no hoes over hurr."

Mudman laughed and nodded his head. "Shut yo' bitch ass up. Nigga, tell me what the fuck going on in dat spot wit' Dirty n'em? I need to know how much dey holding?" He took the Draco off of Prentice and set it beside him before grabbing his bottle of Sprite that he'd poured a sixth of codeine into.

Prentice closed his eyes for a second. He allowed the tar to take over his body. He nodded for a full minute and continued to scratch his injection site. "A whole lotta shit done changed since da last time you stepped feet on dese streets, Mudman. Dese li'l boys out hurr carrying dem choppas now, and dey killing wit' no regard for life." He leaned forward and nodded out.

Mudman slapped his hands together. "Nigga, wake yo' ass up! Time is money!"

Prentice sat up and bucked his eyes. They scanned Mudman, and then proceeded to get low all over again. "Ma'fuckas shooters, Mudman, and dat nigga Bill supposed to be fuckin' wit' them cartel boys out of Mexico City. I don't know how true dat shit is right thurr, but homeboy been caking for about six months now. Got himself a Range Rover and all dat shit, when about a year ago he was rolling that old beat up Lincoln Continental."

Mudman clapped his hands again. "How much in thurr, potna? Mane, I swear to my grandmomma, I ain't gon' ask dat shit no mo'. You best be telling me what's really good." He set the Draco on his lap and aimed the barrel nonchalantly toward Prentice. Mudman was getting angry, and when he got angry, there was very little reasoning or rationalization that took place inside of his brain.

"A little birdie say that ma'fucka just got a whole thang. I'm talking thirty-six zips of that ninety-five percent pure shit that I'm floating on right now. We wind up getting our hands on that, and its gon' be a straight pay off," Prentice assured him. He scooted back on the couch and rested his head between his legs. His nails continued to scratch at the injection site. He was high as a kite being blown by the wind.

Mudman stood up. "How sho' is you 'bout dis shit?"

"Sho' as can be. All my information is firsthand. He got a whole bunch of cash up thurr too 'cause he waiting to cop some of those pills and thangs from the same cartel. My source say he don't go off to Phoenix to cop that shit until tomorrow though, so dat cash gotta be in that club wit' him, mane."

Mudman smiled. "Bet those." He grabbed his light spring jacket from the couch and slid into it. "Well a'ight, mane. I'ma go 'head and let you nod and thangs. I'm finna go handle dis bidness. I'ma fuck wit' you tomorrow." He grabbed the Draco from the couch and hoisted it up against his shoulder.

Prentice opened his eyes and sat back on the couch. "Hold up, potna. Dat's supposed to be my lick, too. I was waiting until you got out before I pulled the plug, but now that you home from serving yo' li'l bid, it's ripe to handle dat shit right now. Just let dis shit wear off a li'l bit and I'll be ready to go, believe dat."

Mudman shook his head. He stepped over to Prentice and stood over him while he continued to nod. He shook his head at his cousin and felt disgusted. He couldn't understand how the man had allowed himself to be conquered by the drug. It was a major sign of weakness, and it cut Mudman deep. He knew he couldn't depend on Prentice when the heat was on, although the man had never failed him in the past, but before Mudman went to prison, Prentice wasn't shooting his heroin, and now he was, and that disgusted him. "Say, nigga, yo' monkey ass staying right thurr in that seat. You ain't coming wit' me no how."

Prentice scooted to the edge of the couch and got up on staggering feet. "Yes, the fuck I am. I need that money just as bad as you do. We supposed to split that shit down the middle. Fuck what you talking about."

Mudman felt his blood beginning to heat up. The scent of Prentice's sweat and unwashed ass annoyed him. He looked down at his cousin and lowered his eyes. "Nigga, you heard what the fuck I said. Sit yo' ass down. Dis my lick, and I ain't finna share it wit' you, or nobody else. Dat's final."

Prentice pulled his nose and took a step back. His high began to leave from him as his anger set in. "Say, Mudman, I know you been gone a long time, but nigga, you must have forgot that my body count stacked as high as yours. You ain't finna hoe me out of nothing. Now I said that I'm coming wit' you because this was my lick way before you even stepped foot on solid gr---"

Mudman swung and hit Prentice with all of his might right in the mouth. Prentice flew backward and fell over the table. He hit the back of his head on the floor and became woozy. He struggled to shake the cobwebs from his head. Before he could, Mudman hopped over the table and straddled him. Mudman grabbed him by the throat and squeezed with his left hand. He balled his right fist. "You simple-ass nigga, I said you ain't going wit' me. You thank I give a fuck 'bout yo' body count? Nigga, I'm broke. Ain't got a pot to piss in, and I need dis money. Now you standing in my way. I'll cut yo' ass in on the next lick, ya feel me?"

Prentice felt the blood leak down the side of his face. Because of the tar, the pain was minimal. He grabbed Mudman's hand from his neck and pushed him off of him. "Get the fuck off of me, mane!" He jumped up and dusted himself off.

Keisha ran into the basement with a Butcher's knife in her hand. "What da fuck going on down here?" she hollered, looking from one man unto the next. When she spotted the blood coming from Prentice's face, she knew that something wasn't right. She turned to Mudman and raised the knife. "Mudman, get yo' crazy ass out of my house! Now!"

Mudman mugged her. "Bitch, shut up. Dis ain't got shit to do wit' you. Dis between me and my cousin."

11

She took a step forward with the knife. Keisha was born and raised in Baton Rouge. She had been around crazy niggas her whole life, and she'd been fighting ever since she was a real little girl. Mudman didn't put fear in her heart. In fact, she hated him. She hated him because wherever he was, death seemed to follow him. She had been against Prentice allowing him to stay with them after he was released from prison. She knew it was going to be a bad idea, and so far, he had proven her right. "Mudman, get the fuck out of my house! Now!" She took a step toward him with the knife again.

"Say, mane, get yo' bitch, Cuz. Dat hoe always running her mouth. Get her li'l black ass or she 'bout to wind up in a creek. Believe dat shit right thurr."

"Nigga, watch yo' ma'fuckin' mouth. Don't be calling my bitch no hoe. Fuck wrong wit' you?" Prentice asked, mugging Mudman.

Mudman stood still. He sized up the couple as his vision began to go hazy. His blood was boiling like water with Ramen noodles inside of it.

"Get out of my house!" Keisha yelled.

That did it. Mudman closed the distance in between them and grabbed Keisha by the throat. He picked her up with one hand and slammed her into the wall as hard as he could, indenting her body into the thin dry wall. A cloud of smoke billowed into the air. "You punk-ass bitch, you always running yo' mouth. You always got somethin to say. I'm sick of dat shit." He choked as hard as he could until his nails were digging into her skin. Blood seeped around his fingernails.

Keisha raised the knife and slammed it into Mudman's shoulder. She twisted it again and again.

Mudman hollered out and dropped her. He released the Draco and placed his other hand over his stab wound as blood gushed through his fingers. "Aww! You punk-ass bitch! I'm finna kill you!" He leaned down to pick up the Draco. His mind was on shooting Keisha. He wanted to send her straight to the morgue. He'd felt that way ever since they were in high school.

Prentice dived and landed on top of the Draco. "Hell n'all, mane, you ain't finna kill my baby mama." He scooped up the gun and took off running up the stairs with it. When he got to the last room in the back of the house, he tossed the gun on the bed and slammed the door before rushing back to the basement again.

Keisha rushed Mudman with the knife and swung it wildly. Her pretty dark-skinned face appeared evil and focused. She was 5'3" tall and 140 pounds, small, but with the heart of a lion. "Get. Up. Out. Of. My. House. Nigga!" She sliced him across the arm and clenched her teeth. If she had to kill him to get him out of her shit, she was cool with that.

Mudman backed all the way up. He felt the slice on his arm, and it excited him. "Fuck you, bitch." He waited until Keisha swung the knife again, then jumped back and punched her so hard that she flew into the washing machine, dropping the knife. She fell to her knees and slowly got back up. Mudman grabbed her neck and lifted her as high as he could into the air before bringing her back down to the concrete. The air exited her lungs and left her gasping. He grabbed the knife from the floor and turned around to look down on her.

Prentice tackled him in the side, and they crashed into the basement wall. The knife slid across the floor. Both men were wrestling to the best of their abilities, grunting,

13

and groaning. Mudman wound up on top of Prentice. He punched him four hard times, knocking him out cold. He straddled him, looking down into his face, before punching him again, hearing something crunch. "Bitch-ass nigga. You always saving these hoes." He got off of him and stood back. Blood leaked out of his wound and dripped off of his fingers.

Keisha slowly made her way to her feet. She wiped her mouth. Her bottom lip was busted. She squinted her eyes and tried to focus in on the big target of Mudman standing before her. As soon as he came into view, she held up her guards. "Come on, muthafucka, I ain't scared of you. Let's do this." She tightened her fist as hard as she could and rushed him, swinging fast and wild.

Mudman blocked two of her blows and grabbed her by the neck again. He picked her up and fell to the ground. He straddled her body, holding her wrists to the concrete of the basement. Keisha kicked wildly and tried to head butt him. The more she tried to fight him, the more excited Mudman became. She humped up into him and tried to buck him off, but it was of no use. Mudman was too strong. He held her for a full three minutes while she worked as hard as she could to free herself. "Let me up, she groaned.

Mudman, leaned down and kissed her juicy lips. He sucked the bottom one into his mouth and licked it. "Mmm, bitch."

This made Keisha furious. She kicked her legs and went all out to break free of him. But her efforts were point-less. "I hate you, Mudman. I hate you. I swear to God I do."

Mudman laughed, looking down on her, then he grabbed her neck hard, shutting off her air supply. "Bitch, da only reason I ain't gon' kill you for what you did to my shoulder is because you got heart, and I like dat shit." He could feel the heat from between her legs warming his stomach. Her thick thighs wrapped around him, trying effortlessly to free herself from him. He'd watched her walk around the house all day long inside of the small Daisy Dukes. And relished how her cheeks jiggled out of the back of them. "Just consider yourself lucky tonight, Keisha." He reached between them and cuffed her pussy, felt its fatness, and groaned before standing up.

Keisha scooted backward on her ass and jumped up. She grabbed the lamp from the table and held it like a baseball bat. "Get out of here, Mudman."

He grabbed his Draco from the floor and waved her off. "Aw, bitch, I'm going." He looked down at Prentice just as the lights went off in their home. Once again, Prentice had neglected to pay the bill. Mudman grunted. "Tell that nigga when he wake up, the job will be done, and I'ma hit his hand." He stepped past her.

As he did, she scurried to the other side of the room. She could still feel his disgusting fingers on her sex. She wanted to kill him. "Never come back, Mudman. I hate you."

Mudman made his way up the stairs and stopped on the third one. He looked down at her. "Bitch, mark my words, before it's all said and done, you gon' be kissing my ass. I promise dat shit."

Hood Rich

Chapter 2

It took Mudman two hours to stitch up his wounds. As soon as they were stitched and patched up, he threw the remainder of the first aid kit inside of his Buick Regency, stepped out into the night, and slammed the door of his car. It was hot and humid. He could hear the crickets somewhere in the distance. He adjusted the .357 Magnum on his waistband and tightened his belt. The handle of the gun rested against his stomach muscles. He pulled his jacket over the handle and made his way down the alley until he got to the back of the small club. The music bellowed outside, a song by the Isley Brothers. The song reminded Mudman of his mother. She'd played it often while he was growing up.

When he stepped into the club, it was packed. A group of four women tried to squeeze by him. They were older and smelled good to him. He'd been down a long five years and had yet to release any of his pent-up frustrations. That was his next priority. He looked around the club and saw that the lights were dimmed. There were four big speakers that allowed for the music to completely consume the small expanse of the club. Couples danced on the floor. The bar was filled with patrons, and bartenders looked busy. Two security guards roamed around the crowd. Mudman slipped past them and found a seat at the end of the bar. He kept his hood pulled over his head.

The bartender, a short, heavyset woman with red skin and brown eyes, stepped across from him. "Baby, what can I get you?" She smelled of cheap perfume and alcohol.

"Nothin yet, shawty, I'm still learning, just gimme a second." He continued to scan the club until he found Bill located in the back booth with a bottle of Moët in his hand. He was surrounded by beautiful women. Two security guards that looked like some locals from the hood stood behind him in black T-shirts.

Mudman got off of the barstool and made his way to the back of the club. Bill's section was roped off by red velvet ropes. As soon as Mudman got close enough, one of the heavyset bodyguards blocked his path and placed his hand on his chest. "Say, mane, where the fuck you thank you going, homeboy?" he asked. He had a toothpick in the corner of his mouth, Mudman assumed to make himself look harder.

Mudman smacked his hand off of him so hard that the security guard stumbled backwards. "Get yo' muthafuckin' hands off of me, nigga. Fuck wrong wit' you?" he snapped. He took another step forward before the other security guard stepped into to his face.

"Sir, you can't cross this rope. This section is private. It's reserved for Mr. Bill Watkins," the 6'5" heavyset, former boxer announced.

Mudman sized him up quickly. His arms were the size of a fat woman's thighs. His bald head looked like a Thanksgiving turkey without its limbs attached. His breath smelled like stale cigarettes and shit. Mudman took a step back. "Say, potna, I'm tryna to holler at the homie right thurr. I got some shit I wanna run by him."

The bodyguard shook his head. "Nall, mane, it don't work like that. You wanna holler at Mr. Watkins, you need to make an appointment. Else you asking for a whole lotta trouble." He clenched his jaw and cracked his knuckles.

The other security guard had taken his place beside the second one. He looked vengeful and angry. Sweat slid down the side of his face. "You heard what he said, and unfortunately, I'ma have to ask you to leave."

Mudman ignored him. He rubbernecked past the two men. "Say, Bill, I need to holler at you real quick. I think I got some shit you wanna get up wit'."

Bill had a thick-ass redbone sitting on his lap. She slowly winded on him, leaned all the way back, and sucked his neck. Bill waved Mudman off. "Get him out of here."

The first security guard went to grab Mudman. Mudman took a step back and upped one of his .357s. He swung the gun and crashed it into the side of his head, shattering his forehead. The man hollered and fell to his knees, holding his face. The girls screamed. The one that had been on Bill's lap jumped up and ran into the crowd. The second security guard rushed Mudman with his head down.

Mudman sidestepped him and fired the gun. The bullet flew from the gun and landed in the man's chest, ripping it open. He twisted and fell backward. Mudman stood over him and fired two more shots, both bullets landing in his face and splashing the floor with blood. The man shook on the floor before his life faded away from him.

Bill jumped up as the clubgoers began to scatter in every direction, creating pandemonium. He reached inside of his suit coat pocket and pulled out a .9 millimeter. By the time he had the chance to look over to Mudman, Mudman had already smoked both of his bodyguards and stood holding two barrels at him. Bill dropped the gun on the floor and held his hands up. "Say, mane, what the fuck is dis all about?"

Mudman jumped over the table and punched Bill in the face, slinging him to the floor. He reached down and picked him up. He placed a gun on his hip, and the other one went crashing through Bill's teeth, causing the man to spit out fragments. Then he slung him over the table. Mudman picked up his .9 and placed it in the small of his back.

Bill slowly came to a push-up position. "What the fuck you want, mane? You don't know who you fuckin' wit." He struggled to get up.

Mudman grabbed him by his dreadlocks and pulled his head backward. "Take me to yo' muthafuckin' stash right now, or I'm snuffing you," he demanded, pulling his head back far enough that Bill could feel his bones popping.

"Okay. Okay, mane. You can have all of dis shit. Just let a nigga live to see another day."

"Shut up and get up," Mudman said, yanking him to his feet.

***

Fifteen minutes later, Mudman pulled up to Bill's two-story house. He jumped out of the Buick and popped the trunk. He reached inside of it and took hold of a bound Bill. "Get yo' ass up. Come on."

Bill was led out of the trunk and through his front door. Mudman took the keys out of his pocket and fixed them into the lock. He scanned the neighborhood and noticed that Bill stayed directly across the street from a swamp. There was a big sign up that read: Beware of Alligators. Lightning bugs flashed through the air. Crickets sounded all around. There was a murky smell of seaweed and funk. After the key twisted inside of the lock, Mudman eased open the door and pushed Bill inside of it.

Bill fell onto the welcome mat. He looked over his shoulder at Mudman, hating the man and praying that he could make it to his .45 that he kept inside of his safe for times such as these. He climbed to his feet and kept his hands where he was sure that Mudman could see them. "A'ight, man, just be cool. You can take everything. All I

20

ask for is my life," he reasoned, once again praying that he could make it to his .45 before Mudman could harm him any further.

Mudman grabbed him around the neck and placed his lips to his ear. "Look, nigga, if I ain't in and out of here in less than five minutes, when they find your body, they gon' call me a psycho." He released his hold and pushed him so hard that Bill flew forward.

Bill stumbled and caught his balance. The smell of Mudman's breath was fresh in his nostrils. "A'ight, we going to the kitchen. My safe is directly behind it. Let me open that ma'fucka, and the sooner you get what you came for, the sooner you can get the fuck out of my shit."

"Tick tock, nigga." Mudman looked at the digital clock, which read 1:02 a.m. He'd already made up his mind that if he wasn't out of Bill's place by 1:07 a.m., he was going to do the man real bad.

Bill hurried to the kitchen. He took ahold of the side of the refrigerator and pulled it away from the wall. Boxes of cereal and Wonder bread fell from atop it. He kicked it out of the way and knelt behind the refrigerator. He removed the bottom piece of wall and exposed the digital safe. He took one look over his shoulder to see how close Mudman was to him and decided that if he played his cards right, he would have enough time to get to his .45 and let off more than a few rounds before Mudman could react. The way he saw it, no matter what he was in a lose/lose situation. If he allowed Mudman to get away with the dope and money, the cartel was sure to kill him with no hesitation. They didn't give a fuck about excuses. It was either you had what belonged to them, or you lost your life. Now, when it came to Mudman, he had already witnessed the man murder two of his bodyguards with no regard for their lives. He knew he wasn't playing, and he figured that if he didn't give him what he came for, Mudman was going to murder him.

"Three minutes, nigga," Mudman reminded him.

"A'ight, a'ight, I got dis." He began to do the code on the safe. After the numbers were punched in, he pressed his finger on the fingerprint reader. The safe took three seconds to read it. Then it beeped five times and popped open with a loud click. "See, I told you. Grab me a garbage bag out of that garbage can. It's a whole lot in here," Bill said, hoping that Mudman would bite the bait.

But Mudman was a veteran at only twenty-three years old. The stick up game had been his way of life ever since he was ten years old and living from house to house with his mother. He stepped forward and pressed his gun to Bill's back. "Open that bitch and let me see what's in it."

Bill nodded. "Okay, dat's cool." It was now or never. He knew he wouldn't be able to get away without being popped. He would take a shot through the back. It was better than one to the head, as long as he would be able to get a shot off on Mudman. He slid his hand into the safe. It bumped the kilo of Sinaloa Tar, and then his fingers slid around the .45.

Mudman shot him in the back. The shell rolled across the floor. "Bitch-ass nigga."

Bill fell backward with the .45 in his hand and aimed it up at Mudman before finger-fucking the trigger. Bocka. Bocka. Bocka. Bocka. "Ahhhhh!" he hollered, busting over and over.

Mudman felt he first two bullets slam into his shoulders, and another bullet crushed his collarbone. He gritted his teeth in pain but stayed the course. He aimed at Bill's face and squeezed. Bocka! Bocka!

Bill felt the second bullet rip through his right eye. The back of his head exploded. The .45 slid from his hand. He could hear it slide across the floor before his heart took one hard beat and stopped altogether. His last sight was of Mudman raising his foot before he was to slam it down with all of his might onto his face, stomping him out.

Mudman stomped him ten times and fell back after seeing that Bill was lifeless. He took a deep breath. He could feel the excruciating pain permeating through him. Blood dripped from the waistband of his pants, but still he refused to be denied. He opened the safe and saw the lone brick of Sinaloa sitting inside of it along with ten thousand in cash. He grabbed the money and the work. He turned the gas on the stove on each eye and opened the oven. Then he rushed into the living room and set the couch on fire before rushing out of the front door, feeling woozy.

Hood Rich

Chapter 3
Two weeks later...

Keisha pulled the patch off of Mudman's bullet wound and looked over the stitches. She shook her head and sighed. "Can somebody please tell me again why I'm here cleansing this nigga's wounds after all the shit he did to me and you, Prentice? This some straight up bullshit right hurr, that's just what dis is." She dabbed at Mudman's shoulder wound with a wet alcohol pad. The scent of his cologne made her stomach turn over.

Prentice staggered into the den and sat on the sofa next to Keisha. She had Mudman on the floor, sitting between her legs while she worked on him. Prentice was high as a kite. He nodded and scratched at himself as he usually did around that time of day. "Baby, you da only one dat's able to do all dis medical shit. If it wasn't for you, da homie would have bled out already." He rested his hand on Mudman's shoulder. "Ain't dat right, Cuz?"

Mudman jerked away from him. "Nigga, what I tell you 'bout all dat lovey dovey shit? Stop touching me," he warned, mugging Prentice. He stared at him for a few seconds and then situated himself back between Keisha's warm thighs. Her perfume was intoxicating. He couldn't help being on hard as he sat between her legs. She was so thick, and so sexily chocolate.

"Damn, Mudman, you be coming down hard on my baby daddy. I'ma need you to ease up a li'l bit, nigga. He the only reason I'm doing any of this shit. I'm telling you dat right now." She rolled her eyes and taped the gauze pad back over his injury.

Prentice waved Mudman off. "Dat fool just is how he is. Don't pay him no mind," he slurred. His eyes rolled to the back of his head, then he was nodding off.

Mudman was once again disgusted. He turned around to face Keisha. From this vantage point, he could see the outline of her pussy lips through the thin material of her booty shorts. He low key inhaled hard to smell more of her. He yearned for a shot of her pussy, and he knew that one way or another, he was going to find a way to get some of it. He didn't give a fuck if Keisha was his cousin's woman or not. That pussy spoke to him. "Say, shawty, even though he up thurr nodding and shit, he right. I don't mean nothin' by it, and on some real shit, I appreciate you for holding me down, even after I did what I did to y'all. That says a lot about your character." He looked into her eyes, and as soon as hers trailed off, he glanced at the camel toe between her baby oiled thighs.

Keisha nodded. "Look, we all fucked up under dis roof. Ain't none of us perfect. I forgave you for what you did, and I let dat shit go. Now if you try it again, I'ma blow yo' shit back, but for now, it's all good. Besides, that five G's you gave me helped out a lot with the bills. We were behind like a muthafucka." She smiled and made him turn back around.

Mudman laid his head back too far and wound up resting it against her pussy. He moved it further into her and turned his head all the way around until his face was in her snatch. Once there, he inhaled her scent and sucked a piece of a lip that was exposed by the crotch band. Keisha pushed him forward and looked over at Prentice, worried that he'd caught sight of what Mudman had just done.

Prentice was slobbering at the mouth. He sat with his head in his lap, snoring slightly. He was gone off a mix of codeine and a gram of Sinaloa. He was fucked up; Mudman had made sure of that.

Mudman positioned himself on his knees and sucked her inner thigh. He licked up and down the side of it while his thumb traced the center of her lips through her tight shorts. After a little manipulating, the crotch turned damp, and a small wet spot appeared right in the center.

"Stop, Mudman. You tripping," she hissed, and then she threw her thick thigh over his head. She stood up and popped back on her legs, looking down on him.

Mudman focused on the gap between her thighs. He saw the way her knees shook. He could tell that she was affected by his touch. He glanced over to Prentice and frowned at her. "Look at that nigga. Come on, man, what's really good?" He stood up and pulled her closer to him. His dick was semi-erect.

Keisha felt it poke her in the stomach. Once again she looked over at Prentice. He continued to snore. She wiggled out of Mudman's embrace. "Get off of me, Mudman. Your fuckin' cousin is right thurr. What's wrong with you? You gotta go." She stood at the bottom of the stairs. "Come on." She waited by them for him.

Mudman grabbed his shirt from the floor and headed over to her. He stepped into her face and looked into her brown eyes. "Shawty, you fine as hell, and I know you feel that electric shit between us. Stop flexing like you don't."

She grabbed him by the arm and moved him out of the way. "Boy, get the fuck out of here, it's time to go." She stepped past him and headed up the stairs. "Nigga, follow me to the door. You done overstayed your welcome."

Mudman peered up the stairs at her. He saw the way her shorts were all in her chocolate ass. Both ass cheeks were exposed and jiggling like Jell-O. He was even able to make out some of her cellulite, and it drove him crazy. Before he could stop himself, he shot up the stairs and grabbed her around the waist. They fell on the top step.

"Get off of me, Mudman, what are you doing?" She turned around and tried to swat him away.

Mudman stuck his face between her thighs from the back and yanked the material to the side. Her pussy popped out at him, and he shivered. The fact that she wasn't wearing panties did something to him. He'd known that fat ass was jiggling too much. He sucked her cat into his mouth and pulled on the left lip. It felt thick and meaty to him.

Keisha arched her back and fell on her stomach. The sensation from his tactics sent a chill up her spine. She got lost for a second, and then she remembered how much she loved Prentice and slapped at Mudman. "Get off of me, boy. Stop. What are you doing?"

Mudman was on brick by this point. He squatted down, picked her up by the waist, and carried her down the hallway. They fell once again in the middle of it, this time with him between her thighs. He held her wrists and sucked all over her neck. The material of her shorts was pulled to one side. Her chocolate pussy was displayed for his eyes. He rubbed into her seam with his right hand, and as soon as she tried to fight him off with her left, he trapped her wrist again, licking up and down her neck, even taking the time out to bite into it with his teeth.

Keisha closed her eyes and tried to hump into him to get him off of her. "Please, Mudman. Please get off of me. Get off of me or I'm going to kill you."

Mudman didn't give a fuck what she was talking about. He had seen her walk around the house in her little shorts with her ass jiggling for long enough. Most of her tops were transparent, and her D-cup titties bounced up and down.

The nipples were prominent, and it made it very easy for him to see her areolas through any blouse or beater that she wore. Keisha was sexy, one of the baddest bitches in Baton Rouge, Louisiana to him.

Mudman slipped his dick out of his jeans and through his boxer hole. He ran it up and down Keisha's crease. She was undeniably soaked down there. As soon as his head felt her heat, Mudman grew another four inches. He slipped past her lips and slammed his dick home. He grabbed her by the shoulders, making her slam down on him.

Keisha squeezed her eyes as tight as she could. She felt Mudman bore into her womb and could not believe that he'd done what he was doing right there in the hallway while Prentice nodded out downstairs. She felt his length opening her wider than she had ever been opened by any man. His length knocked on the door to her G-spot almost immediately, and as good as it started to feel good, she hated him for ruining her purity, her faithfulness to Prentice. "Un. Un. Shit. Get off of me. Puh. Puh. Puh-leeze," she groaned.

Mudman had her thighs on his shoulders, fucking her at full speed. He was fucking her so hard that her titties jiggled out of her pink beater. Both nipples were rock hard and tight. He leaned forward and sucked on each one. Her pussy was tight and wetter than he could have ever imagined. He could tell that he was stretching her. He would pull all the way back and then slam forward, digging deep into her box. Every time he crashed into her, Keisha would emit a moan that she couldn't hold back.

Keisha arched her back and dug her nails into his sides. He was fucking her so hard and fast that she felt like she couldn't breathe. All she could feel was this intense pleasure of being filled like never before, and this degrading feeling of betraying Prentice. It was like eating a whole cake. It may have tasted good in the moment, but she knew that when it was all said and done, she was going to be sick. She felt Mudman bite and then pull on her right nipple with his teeth and she came hard, biting into his shoulder.

Mudman felt her pussy lock up around his piece. He shuddered and came, pumping five years of pent-up frustrations into her. Instead of pulling out, he flipped her on to her knees and got to long stroking her from the back while he watched his dick go in and out of her. The sounds coming from between their sexes was driving him out of his mind. Keisha's big ass continued to crash into his lap, warming it. It felt soft and hot. The cheeks opened and closed with the impact of his thrusts.

Keisha still couldn't believe that he was taking her pussy the way he was. This was that savage shit at its best, she thought. He must have really wanted her. That both scared and excited her. She began to hate Prentice for being hooked on heroin. She hated him for not being there to protect her. She hated him for bringing somebody as vicious as Mudman into their home.

Mudman forced her face to the carpet of the hallway and fucked her as hard as he could, as fast as he could. Keisha came twice again back to back. Her knees got to shaking. She fell on her stomach with him piping away. It felt like he would never stop. When he rolled her on her side and fucked her some more, she passed out for a few seconds and woke up with him nutting deep inside of her. He pulled out and came all over her chocolate sex lips. He rubbed it around with his head and slipped back into her box while she laid on her back with her thighs wide open. Finally, he slow stroked her, looking into her eyes.

Keisha stared at him for a moment, and then closed hers. She felt sick. She had cheated. It was something that she had never done to Prentice before. She was in disbelief. She felt Mudman ease out of her. He rubbed his piece all over her stomach while he rubbed her pussy and stuck the juices up his nose. Then he kissed her neck and stood up. Keisha opened her eyes.

Mudman looked down on her and offered her a helping hand. "Come on, man."

Keisha glanced over at his piece and saw the way it was hanging in front of him like a dark purple elephant trunk. She gasped and couldn't fathom how she had been able to take all of it. "Dat's okay, Mudman, just leave. I think you caused enough damage." She rubbed up and down her slit. She could feel her lips slowly coming back together. Inside, her tunnel was still throbbing from his vicious pounding. She sat up and came to her feet.

Mudman saw the way her shorts were pulled to the right side of her gap. Both lips were exposed and leaking. Her nipples were rock hard. He wanted to fuck her again. He stepped forward and gripped her ass, causing her to yelp.

Keisha remained silent. She simply looked into his eyes. Her heart was beating faster and faster. She took a deep breath through her nose and exhaled.

"Damn, Keisha, I had to have some of you. Yo' li'l ass been driving me crazy ever since we was kids." He rubbed her pussy from the back and poked her front. He was hard again and breathing heavily.

"Mudman, it's time for you to go. I can't believe you really just did me like that. I thought you respected me."

"I do, but I just had to. I had to get that shit out of my system. You too ma'fuckin' fine to be walking around me all strapped and shit. Pussy dis fat supposed to be getting dicked down by somethin like dis." He humped up and down her slit with the head of his pipe.

She closed her eyes and felt herself getting wet again. Keisha had low key always been obsessed with that pussy-taking shit, but whenever she fantasized about it happening to her, it had always been Prentice, never anyone else. Now she felt tainted and lost. Mudman continued to caress and squeeze her ass. That sent more shivers through her. "You gotta go, Mudman. If Prentice wakes up and smells this house, he gon' kill you, and me." She pushed him away and backed up.

Mudman stood there for a second, reluctant. Then he fixed his clothes and nodded his head in agreement. "Awright. I ain't tryna cause no more drama. I'ma grab my bangers, and then I'm up out of here." He brushed past her and headed back toward the den.

"Wait," Keisha said, stepping forward.

Mudman turned around. "What up?"

Keisha stopped in front of him. She could smell his sweat mixed with her perfume. "You ain't gon' apologize for what you just did to me?" She thought it was the least he could do. He had her feeling like shit.

Mudman looked her up and down. He saw her points pressing through her beater and spotted the juice still trickling out of her box and oozing down her legs. He looked into her wanton eyes and snatched her to him. He picked her up and crashed her back into the wall, where he tongued her fine ass down, holding her up by her ass. She breathed heavily into him, moaned when his fingers found her hole and slipped up into her. He ran them in and out with her groaning into his ear until they heard footsteps on the stairs. Then she jumped down and they parted ways, her rushing into the bathroom and him into the living room, where he faked sleep on the couch.

Hood Rich

Chapter 4

"A'ight now, listen carefully, Mudman, dis fool Billups is having dat stupid cake. Dat ma'fucka just got back from Stockton out there in California, and I know for a fact he holding. We gotta take a good look at his ass. We could come up with every bit of fifteen thousand apiece, and three bricks dat we can split down the middle. Da only thang is dat dis ma'fucka is plugged wit' them hittas back out West - at least that's what everybody saying, I don't know fo' sho'. But anyway..." Prentice stopped to scratch his inner arm. "Damn." He was digging his nails into his skin so much that he tore the skin and it began to bleed. That disgusted Mudman.

"Nigga, finish what the fuck you saying," Mudman spat. He crushed two Percocet sixties and formed two lines, taking one to the head.

Prentice continued. "So anyway, we can go in there and hit his ass up, but we can't fuck him up like that. We gotta take it easy, and we gotta buss the pot down with another nigga."

Mudman finished his second line. "mane, what's dat last part you said right thurr?" Mudman honestly didn't give a fuck what Prentice had to say. He wasn't splitting shit with nobody else. He barely wanted to bust it down the middle with Prentice.

"Damn, Cuz, da reason we gotta buss dis shit hurr down is 'cause dis nigga Billup's right hand man is the one putting us up on dis lick. He say his potna been acting real shady ever since he got back from Cali fuckin' with dem Mexicans. Ma'fucka want me to bring 'em back down a few notches."

Mudman sucked his teeth as Keisha walked into the living room with a pair of tight capris on. She bent over and picked up the trash from Prentice's McDonald's. Mudman couldn't help but imagine what it had felt like fucking her from the back only a week prior. He was feening for some of her box again.

"Baby, do you want me to get you somethin' to drank?" she asked, standing up and popping back on her legs.

Prentice waved her off. "Nall, shawty, we on something in hurr right now. Go on out dere and come back in a minute."

"Okay, baby." She continued to grab the trash from around the table. When Keisha got in her cleaning mode, there wasn't nothing that anybody could tell her. She began to sing a song under her breath.

Mudman's dick was so hard watching her ass that it was jumping up and down in his pants. He felt like snatching her ass up and fuckin' her right in front of Prentice. He didn't give a fuck what he would think or try to do. He would cross that bridge when he came to it.

Prentice peeped Mudman's eyes and mugged him. He followed them to Keisha's ass and saw the way her pants molded her monkey. This infuriated him. "Say, mane, do like I tell yo' ass right now. I said we in hurr talking bidness."

Keisha frowned. "A'ight, niggas, damn. I'm gone." She walked away with an armful of their trash.

Mudman watched that ass jiggle until it disappeared. When he looked back across the table, Prentice was glaring at him. "Fuck you mugging me for, nigga?"

"You see something you like?" Prentice asked.

"What?"

"You heard what the fuck I said. I said, do you see something you like? Yo' eyes all on Keisha's ass and shit. Since when you start watching her like that?"

Mudman waved him off. "Nigga, you tripping. You my ma'fuckin' cousin, dat's yo' baby mama. Dat rotten shit ain't in me like dat, homeboy. Shawty my family, just like you are. I might have looked at how she was fitting dem jeans, but it wasn't on no lustful shit. Just think she gained a li'l weight, dat's all," Mudman lied.

Prentice looked him over for a second. He was trying to decide whether or not to believe him, but then again, he knew that Mudman spoke his mind. He knew that he didn't sugar coat shit. Plus, he was aware of Keisha's hatred toward Mudman, and vice versa. He decided that Mudman was, in fact, telling the truth. "Yeah, I thought she was putting on a little weight. I'ma have to get on top of that. Ma'fucka ain't tryna have no fat bitch walking around dis house, you feel me?" Prentice busted up laughing.

Mudman didn't join in. He thought that Keisha's body was perfect, and in addition, big girls were sexy to him. Not that Keisha was anywhere near being a big girl, but still. He let Prentice laugh for a second, and then he clapped his hands together. "Nigga, finish telling me about dis hurr lick."

Prentice cleared his throat. "A'ight, so we can't smoke dis nigga because his right hand mans need him for a bunch of other shit. We just gon' run up in their trap house and lay dem both down. We gon' take everythang. I already got the combinations to the safes and know where the safes are located. Pacer, Billups's right hand man, is throwing a surprise party for Billups tonight. We are already invited. We'll mingle for a minute, and then spin off and mask up.

After we mask up, we gon' lay everybody down and get the fuck up out of dere, you feel me?"

"Yep, sounds good to me," Mudman said, laying back on the couch. He still had Keisha on his mind.

Prentice pulled out his works and started setting up to take his drug. "Mane, dat's like three hours away. I gotta get right." He pulled the Sinaloa out of his front pocket and set it on the table.

Mudman stood up. He knew that this process would take Prentice every bit of a half hour to complete. That didn't include all of the nodding that he was about to do. "Say, mane, dat food running through a ma'fucka already. I'ma step up here and take a nice shit to clear my stomach, den I'ma come back down and fuck wit' you. A'ight?"

Prentice was already pouring his work on a spoon, getting it ready. "Nigga, I don't need no muthafuckin' play by play. You see what I'm doing right hurr."

Mudman waved him off and thought about checking his ass. He slipped upstairs in search of Keisha. He could already smell her perfume. She had Monica's new album bellowing out of the speakers. He stepped into the kitchen, and there was no sign of her. He frowned and peered down the hallway that led to the living room before going down it. He found her bent over the couch, fixing a pillow. He walked up behind her, and pulled her to him aggressively, his hand over her mouth. She screeched into it. Then he was sucking on her neck, humping into her ass.

Keisha moaned and shivered. Mudman had scared the shit out of her. She felt him unzipping her jeans. Then he yanked them to her knees. She felt paralyzed and couldn't understand why she couldn't bring herself to fight him away. He pushed her over the couch and kicked her feet apart, lined himself up, and slid deep into her from the back.

"Uhhhh!" Keisha groaned.

Mudman took ahold of her hips and piped her fast and aggressively. He pulled her back to him, and at the same time he slammed forward, dicking her down. "Dis my pussy now. Dis mine. Dis mine. Dis mine. Dis mine." Faster and faster, harder, and more aggressive.

Keisha grabbed a pillow and bit into it. She screamed as loud as she could while he worked her over. It felt so wrong. So, so wrong. She came and dug her nails into the sofa. Mudman picked her up and bounced her into the air while he fucked her. Her pussy felt like it had gotten tighter. She creamed over him and shook with reckless abandon. Her arms wrapped around his neck. Her ankles locked around his waist as he took her on a journey.

Mudman felt her walls working him over. He crashed into the wall with her and fell to the carpet, stroking her hard. "Aw fuck! Fuck!" He straightened his back and came back to back inside of her, pumping his seed. He pulled out and pulled up her shirt, cumming all over her tummy.

Keisha felt his hot jets warming her skin. She shook and came again. Then she was lying on her back, rubbing her pussy while he stood up and pulled up his pants.

"Damn, baby, you driving a nigga nuts."

She saw his big dick disappear, and a part of her got sad, and she hated herself for feeling that way. Mudman knelt down and choked her with one hand while he sucked all over her lips. This ignited a fire inside of Keisha. She slid two fingers into herself and ran them in and out. Mudman rested his lips on her right earlobe. "Bitch, I'll kill you of you don't give me this box when I want it. Fuck dat nigga Prentice; you belong to me. I'm dat nigga for you.

You hear me?" He squeezed harder, scooted down, and sucked on her clitoris as hard as he could.

Keisha came again. He released her. She jumped into the air on the carpet, cum running down her thighs. "I hate you. I swear I hate you," she muttered, shivering like crazy.

Mudman left her on the floor just like that.

***

Mudman stayed in the far back corner of the party as the partygoers laughed and joked. They popped bottles and passed around dro-filled Cuban stuffed cigars. It was two in the morning and raining like crazy outside. The two-story house was packed. They had already surprised Billups, and the best was yet to come. Mudman felt the Percs drip from the back of his nostrils and into his throat. He brushed his hand past the handle of his .40 Glock and smiled slightly.

Prentice stepped over to him, eating a piece of cake. In the background was the sound of Lil' Boosie, Baton Rouge's very own savage. Prentice leaned closer to his ear. "Say, mane, dat nigga upstairs in the Argos right now counting them bands wit' Pacer. Pacer just texted me and told me it was good to go. You ready?"

"Like a bitch gone off of Mollie. Let's fuck dis nigga over for dat cheese, homie." He nodded for Prentice to take off.

Prentice dumped the cake inside a trash can on the way to the back steps. He put a mug on his face and felt the heroin taking over him. He had never liked Billups, and the lick for him was more personal than he let on. Stripping the dope boy was going to be the best part of his year. He felt like he needed to be brought down a couple notches.

Mudman waited until they got into the dark hallway before he pulled his .40 out, slid his mask over his head, and held his gun against his hip. "Come on, nigga."

Prentice took the steps first. He ascended them. When he got to very top, his mask was already on. He pulled his .357 and rushed the table that Pacer and Billups were sitting at, counting a pile of money that totaled thirty thousand dollars. He got to Pacer fist and flung him to the floor. "Nigga, you already know what dis is. Lay dat ass down," he growled.

Pacer laid on the floor with his arms above his head. "What da fuck!"

Billups went for his gat. Mudman hopped the table and landed on top of him. He turned the gun around and proceeded to beat him senseless, over and over again. Each blow felt like a ton of bricks being crushed into Billups's head. The pain was so intense that he yelped with each hit. He felt his skull crack, and Mudman kept on beating. His jaw was the next to crumble, and then he faded out.

Mudman slammed the handle into him twenty more times. When he stood up, his chest was heaving up and down. Sweat drenched his mask. He knelt back down and went through Billups's pockets, obtaining two more thousand in cash. He ripped the gold Rolex off of his wrist and yanked the chain from his neck. "Bitch-ass nigga."

Pacer looked over to Billups from his position on the floor. He saw all of the blood coming from his right hand man and began to panic. "Aw shit. Aw shit. What da fuck you do?" He jumped up and rushed over to him. He took two fingers and placed them to his neck. He couldn't feel a pulse. He jumped up. "He dead. Dis ma'fucka dead. Y'all wasn't supposed to kill my homeboy," he groaned.

Prentice walked over and looked down. "Damn, mane. Shit!"

Pacer walked back and forth, holding his head. "Why you let him do this shit, Prentice? Y'all took it too far. Shit, I gotta go, fuck dat money." He made his way toward the stairwell.

Mudman blocked his path and pulled his mask off. His gray eyes penetrated those of Pacer's brown ones. "You ain't taking yo' monkey ass nowhere." He took a step back and smiled.

Prentice stepped in front of Pacer and grabbed the back of his head. He forced his cheek to meet that of his .357 before he pulled the trigger twice. Pacer's brains splashed across his face. He could feel the hot meat before it dropped off of his skin and to the floor. He stood over him and dumped two more rounds into his body, then he and Mudman grabbed what they came for and fled out of the back of the party.

Chapter 5

It was two-thirty in the afternoon, three days later. Keisha was waiting on the bus stop, preparing to go to her second job at Walmart, where she was assistant manager. The sun was high in the sky. It was hot and humid, mid-August, and roasting. She wiped her sweat away with her hand and fanned herself. "Damn, where dis bus at? Dis ma'fucka every bit of twenty minutes late."

As she was looking one way down the road in search of the city bus, Mudman was rolling down the street in his black Benz. He saw her and made a show by slamming on his brakes and hitting a U-turn in the middle of the street. He stepped on the gas and sped up, then slammed on his brakes again. The other people that were waiting on the bus stop had run away, thinking that they were about to be under attack. Keisha stayed put and crossed her arms with her work bag draped over her shoulders. She looked disinterested. Mudman rolled down the black-tinted windows. "I'm saying, shawty, why you ain't running like they scary ass?" he asked, his mouth full of gold.

She smacked her lips. "For what? It's already preordained when I'm finna die. Fuck I look like running away from death?"

That response made Mudman's piece twitch. He loved when females had heart. "Say, shawty, fuck dat job, you rolling wit' me today. I'ma spend some money on you," he said, holding up a knot of hundreds. "Most of dis shit fa you guh."

Keisha ignored him and kept looking for the bus. She didn't want to give in to his temptations. She already knew what Mudman had up his sleeve. It would be more of the usual. She wished that she had never crossed those lines with him. Every day she felt like telling Prentice what had happened between her and his cousin. She was already having a hard time looking Prentice in his eyes. "Boy, I ain't fuckin' wit' you. You thank I'm 'bout to lose my steady job over one li'l trick session? Nigga, please. Dis my only stability right hurr. Prentice been slacking." Shoot. She didn't even mean to say that last part. It had slipped out. She looked past him again and saw that her bus was finally coming. She sighed. "Mudman, I'll see you later."

Mudman looked into his rearview mirror. He saw the city bus fast approaching, and it irritated him. He hated rejection. He hated when anybody made him feel less than a boss. He flared his nostrils and backed his Benz up into the spot that the city bus was set to stop in order to pick up its new paying riders.

The bus got directly behind him and blew its horn. The driver pushed his window back and stuck his head out of it. "Say, man, move that car, I got a job to do," the dark-skinned, heavyset older man yelled.

Mudman ignored him. "Keisha, come fuck wit' me shawty. Let a ma'fucka spend some money on yo' fine ass. It's the least I can do. Ain't nobody else trying to do dat shit." Mudman knew he was low blowing his cousin, but he didn't give a fuck. He was loyal to nobody.

Keisha felt that slug, and it annoyed her. She waved him off and jogged to the bus. The driver opened the door and let her on. She walked toward the back of the bus and took a seat. The bus was slightly crowded. It appeared that everybody was looking at her like she was crazy. "Damn, mane, fuck all y'all looking at?" She rolled her eyes and turned her nose up.

Mudman threw on his hazards and wound up knocking on the bus's double doors. The driver apprehensively opened them. Mudman flicked a twenty dollar bill in his face and kept walking. He bumped a bigger, light-skinned man out of the way before he sat in the seat in front of Keisha and turned around to face her. "Say, shawty, why you making me go through all of dis?"

"Li'l brother, you gon' have to move yo' car so I can get out. This bus is faulty. It don't go in reverse for some reason."

Mudman stood up and mugged him. "Say, nigga, I ain't going no muthafuckin' where, and I ain't moving shit until she come wit' me. If you move this bus or ask me one more question, I'ma slay every ma'fucka on hurr. Now test me," he hissed feeling his blood boil.

Keisha stood from her seat and grabbed his arm. "Come on, Mudman, before yo' ass winds up in dem white folk's jail." She pulled him to the rear exit, and they departed.

***

They had been rolling for five minutes in silence when Keisha broke it. She'd been staring at him the whole time wondering what was going on in his head. "Mudman, let me ask you a question? Do you mind?"

He reached and turned down the Tupac album. "Nall, shawty, go on 'head." He drove his steering wheel with his left hand, and kept his right hand resting on top of his .40 Glock. Mudman had a lot of enemies, so he was always on the ready to squeeze his pistol until it was empty.

"What da hell was going through yo' head when you just got on dat damn bus back thurr?" She was really curious.

Mudman laughed. "I don't like all dat rejection shit. I'm tryna fuck wit' you for a minute, and hurr you is tryna play me to the left. Dat shit wasn't finna go down."

Keisha scoffed. "Nigga, you lucky I didn't wanna see yo' crazy ass back in jail, or else I would have let you stand yo' stupid ass thurr until dem peoples came. Why you sweating me so hard anyway?"

"I ain't sweating yo' ass. It's just like I said. I just wanted to fuck wit' you for a minute." He kept cruising.

"Boy, why did you make us cross dese damn lines? Don't you know I love yo' cousin wit' all my heart?" She was starting to feel remorseful again.

"Yeah, shawty, I do, but dat ain't got shit to do wit' what I'm tryna do right hurr. You can still love dat nigga, and fuck wit' me too. Ain't nobody tryna drag yo' ass down the altar." He curled his upper lip and got irritated. He didn't like competing with no man, even if it was Prentice. He knew that Keisha belonged to his cousin, but Mudman didn't give a fuck. He was a conqueror by every means, and Keisha was so appealing to him because she was so heavily involved with his people.

"Mane, you making me do shit I ain't never done before. Dat hoe shit ain't in me, Mudman. I'm a good girl. I'm in dat church, for real. That Bible don't play about all dis infidelity and stuff, mane. It say can't nothin' good come from it."

Mudman nodded his head. "Shawty, you can believe what you believe, just don't try and push dat shit off on me. I'm living minute by minute. An hour ain't promised to me, and I know for damn sho' a whole-ass heaven ain't either. Bottom line, I like you. I used to hate yo' ass 'cause you use to run yo' mouth way too much, but now I like you.

Since I do like you, you gon' fuck wit' me. You ain't got no choice. It's simple as dat." He looked over at her.

Keisha was offended. "Nigga, you don't run me. If I don't wanna fuck wit' you, I ain't. And I'm telling you right now that I love Prentice. I gotta be faithful to his ass from hurr on out."

Mudman smiled and ignored that dumb shit she was talking. He didn't wanna hear that shit. He was too busy lost and in his own head. "Shawty, you got some of the sexiest dark skin I done seen in my whole life. Every time the sun hit it, it just look so good. Den dem eyes. Mmm. Mmm. Mmm. Swear to God, you bad. I ain't even gotta mention yo' body. You got me, doe. Straight up. Ain't never paid attention to you like I have been, until most recently."

Keisha looked out of the passenger's window. She couldn't help appreciating his compliments. It had been so long since Prentice had given her any. "What made you start looking at me all crazy and thangs?"

"When I first got home, and you stabbed me wit' dat damn butcher knife. I saw dat killa shit in you, and it piqued my interest. I love when hoes be having heart like niggas do."

"I ain't no hoe."

"You know what I mean, shawty."

She kept quiet and sighed. She didn't know what to think. A part of her felt so scared around Mudman. He was a loose cannon. She never knew what was going to take place or what he was going to do next, and that was terrifying. At the same time, she could genuinely tell that he cared for her, in his own way. She liked that. She liked the way he looked at her. He looked at her as if he was staring at the most beautiful woman in the whole wide world. She hadn't seen that look in Prentice's eyes in a very long time, and that saddened her.

"Why my cousin call you his baby mama if y'all ain't got no kids together?" Mudman asked, turning into the business district of Baton Rouge.

She shrugged her shoulders. "I don't know. I guess it's just wishful thinking." She ran her fingers through her hair and felt that she had more new growth in her micro braids than she liked. It was time to get a new 'do, but with the bills being behind like they were, she didn't know how she was going to be able to manage that.

Mudman peeped her face go sad. He reached over and turned her chin toward him. "What's da matter, li'l one?"

She yanked her chin away. "Nothin'. I just wanna know what we about to be doing? I need to call my job before they fire me."

"You ain't working thurr no more. I got you. You ain't finna be working in no punk-ass Walmart when I'm out hurr laying down the whole muthafuckin' city. Huh, dis you." He tossed her a three thousand dollar knot. It was thirty percent of the money he had, but he was confident in his stick up game. He would get those three G's back by the end of the night. He didn't give a fuck what he had to do.

Keisha thumbed through the money. When she saw that it was all hundreds and fifties, her eyes got bucked. "Mudman, you can't give me all dis, mane. I ain't got no way of paying yo' ass back."

He laughed. "Shawty, you a dime. A dime supposed to have that bag at all times. It's 2019. That broke shit ain't cute. Fall back and let me do me. Tuck that paper."

Keisha held it for a little while longer, and then slid it into her work bag. "Thank you." She looked back out of her passenger's window.

Mudman kept rolling. He felt he didn't need to acknowledge her for saying thank you. After all, she had patched him up and not told Prentice how they had gotten down behind his back. She was a good girl, and he knew it. He felt she deserved a little cash, especially since he and Prentice were robbing Baton Rouge like crazy.

***

An hour later, Keisha had five bags of new designer clothes and shoes that he had purchased. She had three thousand dollars in her purse, and Mudman had already booked and paid for her hair appointment. She felt good and was thankful. She couldn't help smiling. She looked over to Mudman and touched his arm as he was pulling the car over a block away from her and Prentice's home. "Thank you again, Mudman. You didn't have to do any of dis, but you did. I really do appreciate it.

Mudman nodded. "Look, shawty, I already know that you love the hell out of Prentice. Dat's cool. I ain't gon' break up y'all happy home. From hurr on out, I'ma fall back and let y'all be happy.

Keisha's eyes lit up. "You fa real?"

He nodded. "Yeah."

She leaned across the console and hugged him. "Thank you Mudman. You don't have any idea how hard you was making it for me. I love my man. I been one hunnit to him ever since we been together."

Mudman smiled. "It's good." The scent of her caused him to become aroused. He tried his best to ignore it. He didn't even know what he was doing until he pulled her all the way on top of his lap. She straddled him, and he looked into her brown eyes. She looked so sexy. He held her face and kissed her lips softly at first. "Last time, shawty. Dis da last time, I promise." Then he sucked on her lips with more passion while he held her forty inch ass in his hands.

Keisha closed her eyes and relented. All she kept dwelling on was the fact that he said this would be the last time. So, she gave in. She gave in and found herself lost in his kisses. He sucked on her neck and slid his hands under her shirt, yanked her bra cups down before tweaking her sensitive erect nipples. She moaned.

Mudman wanted to fuck her bad. Her pussy was calling out to him, but he knew that it would be all wrong. If he spent a bag on her and fucked, it would erase the emotional aspect for her, and that he couldn't risk. He had to stay the course. He broke the embrace and kissed her neck one last time. "A'ight, shawty, let's get you home."

Keisha slid off of his lap, hot and bothered. She hated herself for the feeling, but she couldn't deny it. She had to get home. Once there she could seduce her man and try to rekindle some of the old flames that the two of them used to possess. All of her parts ached. "Yeah, let's do that, Mudman."

Chapter 6

When Mudman pulled up to the house, Prentice was just pulling up in a black van with four dudes inside of it. He hopped out and came to the driver's side of Mudman's whip. "Say, mane, we need to holler, Cuz."

Keisha slipped out of the car and grabbed all of her bags, before closing the back door. She scurried around the car and kissed Prentice on the lips. "Hey baby."

He returned her kiss and gave her a quick hug. "Hey bae, let me holler at Mudman real quick. I'll be in the house later on." He squeezed her ass and patted it. "Go on now."

"Okay." She took a step away, then stopped and leaned into him. "Daddy, I want some of you tonight. I'ma be ready when you get home. What time is dat gon' be?"

"'Bout one or two. I'll call first."

"Okay." She hurried into the house. She could tell that Prentice had something serious to talk to Mudman about, and she didn't want to hold them up.

Mudman slid from the Benz and stood in front of Prentice. "What's good?"

Prentice looked him over. "Say, mane, we got a problem. You remember dat whole li'l move against Billups and Pacer, and all dat shit thurr?"

Mudman nodded. "What about it?"

"Dem ma'fuckas really was dealing wit' dem Sinaloa Cartel niggas down thurr in Mexico. They done sent some killas to murder me, you, and Keisha. But here's the kicker: they ran into the wrong house and killed the wrong people." Prentice wiped the sweat from his forehead. He looked nervous and afraid.

Mudman pulled his pistol from his waistband and cocked it. "Where dey asses at? We can go handle dese Mexican ma'fuckas right now."

"Dat's the thing. Day ain't send no Mexicans. Ma'fuckas saying dat ain't how they come. They usually use ma'fuckas from yo' own hood or city, mane. They use ma'fuckas that dey got working for them chasing dat bag. So, it can be anybody. All dese niggas down hurr in Baton Rouge done formed their mini cartels up under the major one back in Mexico, and dem real Mexicans funding that shit. I guess in exchange, the smaller cartels gotta do whatever the big ones say. So, it can be anybody."

Mudman kept calm. "I been gone five years, mane. I don't know dese niggas down hurr no more. You done kept yo' ear to the streets, you should know who fuckin' wit' who."

"Oh, I do, for the most part. I got some of my young potnas wit' me, and we finna go asking questions." He turned around and nodded at the van.

Mudman saw four heads with red rags pulled across half of their faces. He felt a murderous chill go through him. "Dem li'l niggas pop that iron?"

Prentice nodded. "You muthafuckin' right."

Mudman continued to mug the van. "I only see four heads. Dat's all the li'l niggas you got?"

Prentice shook his head and swatted away a big-ass mosquito. "It's mo' where dey come from. I got about fifteen mo'."

"Good, 'cause I'm finna test yo' first four. Let's roll into the arboretum over thurr on Creek Way. I'll meet you over thurr." Mudman hopped into his Benz and pulled off. In his mind, it was real easy to find out if a nigga was a killa or not. He didn't have time to play games. He needed savage-hearted killas around him. He had been locked up with about ten Sinaloa Cartel members, and they were brutal. He literally watched one of the men shred a man in the cell directly across from him in Angola. The guards walked past and saw what was going on and kept it moving. Mudman knew that if they were dealing with the same people, then they were in for a war. He picked up speed and wound up getting to the swampy Arboretum just as the sun was finished setting.

Prentice pulled up with his van of savages. They parked behind Mudman's Benz and got out of their whip. The area they were in was surrounded by trees and water. In the background was a seaweed-infested swamp. There were so many bugs that all of the men present continued to smack their skins because of the bugs crawling on them - all of them except Mudman. He was laser focused on the four teens that were standing before him. He was looking to detect any form of bitch in any man.

Prentice stood before his little crew and looked from them back to Mudman. "Say, Rounds, dis my nigga Mudman right hurr. Dis nigga be 'bout dat life fa real. I'm sho' y'all done heard of him before."

All of them shook their heads but kept silent. Mudman walked up to them and pulled out his .40. "Y'all ma'fuckas li'l killas, or straight bitches?"

They looked at each other, confused. Prentice stepped up. "Say, Mudman, dey cool. I done already told you dat shit."

Mudman moved him out of the way. He snatched the teen closest to him. He looked every bit of 6'4" tall and was dark-skinned. "What's yo' name, shawty?"

"Figgady."

"Figgady, huh?

"Yeah, Round, dese my potnas, they run under me."

"You love yo' niggas?" Mudman asked.

"With all my heart. I'll blow somethin down for dem."

"Dat right?" Mudman inquired.

"Dat's muthafuckin' right."

Mudman stepped into his face. "Nigga, is you a bitch, or a cold-blooded killa? Killas ain't got no hearts."

Figgady looked into his eyes and clenched his teeth. "Bitches get walked on leashes or fucked by my crew. I'm a muthafuckin' killa. Test dis shit of you want to."

"Oh, I want to." He handed Figgady the Glock. "Smoke dat nigga right thurr."

Figgady turned around to see who he was pointing at. When he saw that it was one of his homeboys that had just become a part of the circle, one that he wasn't too familiar with, he raised the gun, aimed, and before he could fire, his guy took off running. Figgady chased him. He ran as fast as he could stopped and fired.

His bullets zipped across the arboretum and slammed into the boy's back, punching a hole into him and ripping through his heart. He was dead before he hit the ground. Figgady rushed over to him and grabbed him by the ankle. He dragged him over to Mudman and dropped him. "Like I said, test me if you want to." Figgady respected Prentice. He knew that Prentice was a killa, and he had heard the war stories surrounding Mudman. In Baton Rouge, Mudman, was a legend to be reckoned with. Figgady wanted in by any means. Being in with Mudman and Prentice meant that he would surely be eating off of the land ten times more than he already was. That jack boy shit ran hot in his bloodstream.

Mudman stepped into his face. "I like you. You rolling wit' me." He snatched his gun out of his hand. "Now look at your crew. How many other ones standing dare got that killa shit in 'em?"

Figgady didn't hesitate. "Both of dem. They got the same amount of bodies under they belt as I do. We hunters. "

Mudman nodded, looking them over. "Good, 'cause dat's what I'm forming. I'm forming a crew of hungry savages that's down to murder and slice heads off. We stripping everything moving. Not just hurr in Baton Rouge, but all over the country. You li'l niggas ready to eat, den we finna do just that. But first things first, we gotta clean up our home. Any ma'fucka that even look like dey burping, we finna strip they table away from them. Right here, and right now, I am officially launching us as Cartel Killaz."

Prentice stepped beside him and upped his twin .9s. "You li'l niggas hurr dat shit, huh?"

Figgady and his crew shook up and nodded their heads. "Mane, I got like five other hittas dat's 'bout that life. Let me get my ma'fuckas together, and we gon' do dis shit hurr da right way, believe dat." He pulled two Desert Eagles off his waist, and upon seeing him up his gats, the two standing members of his crew did the same.

Prentice placed his hand on Mudman's shoulder. "Nigga, what you got in mind?" he whispered only loud enough for him to hear him.

Mudman shook his hand off. "We finna eat every nigga in dis city dat thank they in a cartel. Sooner or later, we'll make our way up the ladder. Ma'fuckas thought they murdered us, right?"

Prentice nodded. "Yeah, they coming for us, dawg."

"A'ight den, we finna see about dat," Mudman said, looking off into the swamp as three alligators fell beneath the water.

***

That night when Prentice, got home, Keisha was waiting up for him. She stood by the bed in their room, dressed in a short red negligee that stopped at the top of her thighs. The top was see-through. Her brown areolas were prominent. The room smelled of her perfume. She had only the lamp light on, with candles lit all around. As soon as Prentice stepped through the door, she turned the lamp off.

She came across the room and stepped in front of him. "Hey baby, you're finally home." She took his light jacket off his shoulders and hung it up. Then she grabbed both of his guns and slid one under his pillow and the other into his nightstand before standing back in front of him.

Prentice smiled. He tried to open his eyes as far as he could, but he was fucked up. He'd just done eight ounces of codeine, and two grams of ninety-five percent pure Sinaloa. He was lifted. He scratched his inner arm. "Damn, baby, you look good as a muthafucka. You did all dis shit fa me?" he asked, staggering on his feet.

Keisha helped to steady him. "Yeah, bae, I just been missing you. It's been a while since we did our thing, so..." She looked up to him and peered into his eyes.

Prentice squeezed his eyelids together. "A'ight, shawty, bet those. You betta get ready, 'cause I'm finna smash yo li'l ass." He staggered backwards and pulled his shirt over his head. He flung it to the floor.

Keisha caught a scent of his body odor. It smelled like he hadn't had a shower in a few days. She scrunched her nose. "Damn, baby, you a li'l rank, ain't you?"

He sat on the bed and pulled his pants off. He flung them on top of his shirt. "Shawty, you already know how it is when a ma'fucka grooving. That heroin stay in my system stronger when that dirt clogs my pores up." He stood up and made his way over to her. "You know you like my funk anyway. I know I love yours." He pulled her to him.

The aggressiveness of it all sparked something in Keisha's lower belly. She was trying her best not to focus on the fact that her man smelled ripe. She took a deep breath and calmed herself. "Yeah, you right, boo. But don't you think we should start dis off in the shower together?"

Prentice shook his head. "Nall, shawty, we good." He kissed her lips.

Keisha closed her eyes and tried to allow for herself to fade away into the bliss that was her man. She knew that she loved Prentice with all of her heart and soul. She had ever since they were kids. She melted into his embrace and kissed him back, though she couldn't help focusing in on the taste of nicotine. She'd always hated that he smoked cigarettes, amongst other things. She hated his heroin use as well, but that was a topic of depression for another day.

Prentice grabbed her ass and kneaded it like dough. "Damn, shawty, I miss this ass. Daddy need you to get him hard, doe." He took a step back and dropped his boxers. The scent of his unwashed flesh was prevalent. He stroked his piece. "Shawty, go 'head and suck on this ma'fucka fa me."

Keisha backed up. "What? Hell N'all, baby, I ain't putting that dirty dick in my mouth. We need to shower, baby, you don't smell so good." Her stomach began to turn.

Prentice ran his hand over his face. He opened his eyes wide, and then closed them back. The heroin was taking a toll on him, and the codeine acted as a bully to his brain. It made everything slow down. "Suck dis piece, shawty, I ain't gon' ask yo' ass again."

Keisha backed up and waved him off. She turned on the lamp and sat on the bed. She covered her face with her hands. Tears began to sail down her cheeks. "What happened to us, Prentice? Why are we like dis?"

Prentice grabbed his boxers from the floor. "I don't know what the fuck you talking 'bout. I ain't did shit. You da one tripping."

Keisha shook her head. "It's not just me. That dope got you fucked up. You are not the man I remembered falling in love with."

"You ain't the bitch I remember falling in love wit' neither, but I made my piece wit' dat shit. Life goes on. It ain't all about love anyway, shawty. Ma'fuckas can't live on love alone."

"But it helps," she whispered.

Prentice stood up. "Mane, a ma'fucka ain't got time fa none of dis bullshit right hurr. You had dis room set up like dis right hurr when I came home. Ain't nobody asked you to do all dis, den when I try and move in on yo' ass, you getting to acting all funny cause I smell a li'l different. Dat's dat bullshit right thurr."

"Honey, you stink. You already know I'll do anythang to yo' body. All I'm asking is that we wash up first. Please, I need you," she whimpered. Keisha needed him because she was starting to crave Mudman. She was imagining what it felt like to be with him. To inhale his scent. He smelled so manly, so fresh, so good, and it didn't help that his aggressive dick game was on point. It made her feel so guilty. What type of woman fell for her man's cousin, she wondered to herself? She prayed that her infatuations for Mudman were strictly carnal, and that her love for Prentice had not waned. They had been through so much together.

Prentice sighed and settled on the bed. "Shawty, I know I been fuckin' up. I'ma get myself together real soon and move us up out of Baton Rouge, you gon' see." He sniffed under his arms and laughed. "Damn, a nigga do smell foul as hell. We ain't gotta do shit tonight. I'm too fucked up anyway." He crawled up the bed and laid on his back. "Wake me up at about six-thirty. Good night." He was literally snoring a minute later.

Keisha sat on the edge of the bed with her hands covering her face. She was heartbroken and didn't know what to do, so instead of panicking, she slid to her knees and prayed to God for strength and understanding.

Hood Rich

Chapter 7

Mudman sat on the windowsill of the Jeep Grand Cherokee with a ski mask over his face as Prentice stormed down Jackson Street, where the Dime Bag Cartel were posted selling dime bags of rock cocaine. They'd purchased their shipments from a source back West, and the Cartel Killaz didn't know if it was Sinaloa or not, but they were taking no chances.

Figgady slammed a hunnit round clip into his Mach .90 and cocked it. He rested his elbow on the windowsill and cheesed under his mask. He'd never liked one single member of the Dime Bag Cartel. They hustled three blocks over from his house, and he hated it. More than once they had approached his mother and asked her if she wanted to buy some of their product. One of them, whom she refused to identify, had even grabbed her arm on an occasion. So, this mission was sweet as Kool-Aid for Figgady.

Two of Figgady's homeboys were also sitting on the windowsills of the Jeep, armed with handguns. Prentice stepped on the gas and sped up. He swerved and slammed on the brakes right in front of a group of twenty Dime Bag niggas. Errrrrr-uh! Smoke emitted from the tires.

Mudman opened his eyes wide and began to fire rapidly from his choppa. Bocka-bocka-bocka! Bocka-bocka-bocka! Bocka-bocka-bocka! His bullets shot out of his barrel and slammed into his targets. Some hit necks, others torsos. In a matter of seconds, the ground was painted with blood from his rivals, and he kept right on chopping, busting through the scope of the top of the gun.

Figgady was busting with his tongue out. Every time he saw a splatter of blood, it excited him. He aimed for heads. The Dime Bag crowd had very little time to disburse. They tripped over each other as more and more shots rang out. Then the other two members of Figgady's crew jumped out of the Jeep and looked over bodies, smoking them on sight if they moved in the slightest. After confirming the fifteen body massacre, they jumped back into the Jeep. Prentice stormed away from the curb with a loud screeching sound coming from the tires.

***

Later that night, Mudman sat across from a lightskinned heavyset man by the name of Junkie. Junkie was an arms dealer. Any type of gun, whether hand or assault rifle, you needed it, and he got it. He had been one of the reasons that Baton Rouge was flooded with artillery. He looked across the table at Mudman as the dark-skinned sistah began to serenade the club with a jazz number from Louie Armstrong. The lights were low, and the club took upon a somber appeal. It was peaceful.

Mudman was leaning like a muthafucka. He was gone off of eight ounces of pure codeine. He mouth tasted of medicine. He craved something sweet, and he was struggling to keep his eyes open. He assessed the club for security. Junkie had two bodyguards behind him, and that was all he made out. Mudman had members of his Cartel Killaz stationed all around the club. They were fucked up off of Mollies and Promethazine.

"So, mane, what you talking 'bout, shawty? What you tryna cop from me right now?" Junkie asked, taking a sip from his tea with his pinky out.

Mudman didn't like his voice. It sounded too feminine to him. He wondered if Junkie was a li'l funny, but then thought that it was none of his business if he was. "I need dem choppas, homeboy. I'm tired of shooting dem hand pistols. Ma'fucka need something to set the city on fire, dat's what I need right thurr." Mudman fought to keep his eyes from closing.

Junkie sized him up quick. He had heard a little bit about Mudman, but he wasn't sure how much he could really value him to have monetarily. He wondered if his chips were up or down. "I got a new shipment of Tech .9s in, fresh from the military. They take thirty in the clip, but the clips can be extended to fifty. They got a low jamming factor, and a ninety percent accuracy rating up to eighty yards or closer. Spit three bullet with each tap of the trigger and come equipped with a beam attached that emits a blue light."

"How much we talking?" Mudman asked, watching a thick-ass Puerto Rican walk past with her skirt hugging her like a second skin.

"Two grand a piece. I got ten of them, so that's twenty large." Junkie took another sip from his tea. He watched Mudman carefully to see if he would flinch at the price. He would have easily unloaded them for a G apiece. His connect only wanted five apiece, but he figured, why would he settle for a five hundred dollar profit, when he could make a fifteen hundred dollar profit from each gun?

Mudman scratched his head. "Twenty seems a li'l steep, playboy. How about I give you seventeen bands even for everythang?"

Junkie set his cup of tea on the table. "It sounds like this here meeting is over." He got ready to stand up.

Mudman held up a hand. "A'ight, man, twenty is cool. But I need dis shit by Friday. Me and my potnas going out of town, and we got some bidness to handle.

Junkie, waved him off. "I don't need to know how the sausage is made. Just meet me at A&P's refrigerator store, tomorrow night, at eleven o'clock. You bring my money, and I'll bring da guns."

Mudman rose from the table. "A'ight, I'll be there."

***

Keisha was downstairs in the basement folding clothes, singing to the HER song on her phone, when Mudman, came down and scared the shit out of her. She jumped and dropped the pants she was folding on the floor. "Damn, Mudman, don't be sneaking up on me, dat shit ain't cool." She snatched the pants from the floor and slung them on top of the washing machine.

He laughed and came from behind his back with a single red rose.

She frowned, took the rose, and off of instincts, sniffed it. It smelled sweet. She smiled. "Why you giving me a rose?" She sniffed it again.

"Shawty, I don't know. I just always seen ma'fuckas giving bitches that type of shit in the movies, and it made the females like dem, and all dat type of shit. So, I guess dat's that I'm tryna do." He blushed and felt soft as hell for doing so. He needed to smoke something, that's how he felt. He literally needed to kill a nigga so he wouldn't feel so soft for giving Keisha a rose.

Keisha kept the rose to her nose. "First of all, I ain't no bitch, and second of all, dis is real life. Thirdly, you're only supposed to give a rose to a girl that's yours, or one that you hope to be yours. I belong to yo' cousin, remember?"

"Yeah, I do. But still and all, dat's for you. You deserve it for being so ma'fuckin' fine, and for keeping this house together. I might be in these streets, but I know a Queen when I see one." He leaned forward and kissed her forehead, directly in the center.

Keisha closed her eyes and fought the urge to wrap her arms around his waist. Instead, she backed up and smiled weakly. "Well thank you, Mudman, I really needed a little pick me upper, and you did that." She set the rose beside the pile of clothes and went back to folding them. "So, what you got going on tonight?" she asked, looking him over from the corners of her eyes.

"Shit, probably gon' get some sleep," he lied, knowing that as usual, he was on business to further his Cartel of Savages.

"Oh, dat's what's up." She looked back down to her clothes that needed folding.

Mudman watched how her ass jiggled in her tight skirt. He might have been tripping, but it looked like her ass had grown just a tad over the past few weeks. He imagined what they would look like without the material covering them and became aroused. Before Keisha could move, he was behind her, squatting down. He yanked her skirt up and moved her feet apart. His fingers, wrapped around the thin strip of the thong that separated the cheeks of her ass. He yanked it with all of his strength.

"Uhhhh!" she groaned.

Then his face was in her crease, eating her from the back like a starving lesbian. Her pussy was fat. The lips were engorged in seconds, and then her flower opened up. Mudman ran his tongue in and out of her at full speed before sucking on her clit.

Keisha raised up to her tippy toes. She knocked the clothes off of the washer and moaned deep within the back of her throat. Her eyes were closed tightly. "Uhhhh, shit. Shit. Shit. Shit." She spaced her feet.

Mudman held her open by spreading her cheeks. She had two holes of pink looking back at him. His tongue darted in an out of both holes before he slid two fingers into her and worked them into her pussy at full speed. "Cum on my fingers, Keisha. Cum on 'em. Do it, shawty. Come on!"

Keisha bounced back into his fingers over and over. She held the sides of the washer. Cream oozed out of her. "Please, Mudman. Awww fuck, please."

Mudman's fingers were a blur. They were going in and out of her so fast that he missed her hole twice and had to slide them back into her. "Cum, Keisha. Cum before I choke yo' ass."

That did it. She imagined him choking her, and that pushed her over the edge. She came all over his fuckin' fingers. "Uhhhh, shit!"

As soon as her pussy started to suck at Mudman, he pulled his fingers out and stood up. He unzipped his pants and slid into her hot womb, grabbed her hips, fuckin' her fast and deep. He was reaching for her belly button. "Uh. Keisha! Damn, bitch. Dis my pussy. Dis mine." He sped up the pace and got to fuckin' her so hard that the washing machine began to move backward.

Keisha closed her eyes for a second, then she opened them and looked back at Mudman. He was focused on the sight of his black piece going in and out of her. She licked her lips and came again.

Mudman grabbed a handful of her hair and pulled her head backward. He got to long stroking her to the best of his abilities. Her pussy was so good that he couldn't help groaning. "Throw dat ass back, shawty! Fuck me like I'm fuckin', you," he demanded.

Keisha followed his orders. She was throwing her ass back so hard that she was hurting herself. Mudman was going deeper than he had ever been before, and she craved more of him. He reached under her body and pinched her clit. She came again and buckled.

Mudman caught her, turned her around, and picked her up. He reinserted himself and bounced her up and down on his dick. The Percocets had completely taken over now. He was fuckin' on complete beast mode. "Arrrrrgh!" he growled, slinging her up and down on his dick.

Keisha was slobbering at the mouth, in sexual heaven. Her nipples were so hard that they felt like they were about to pop off as Mudman, took her for the ride of her life.

***

Prentice stumbled into the house and crashed into the wall. He allowed for it to keep him up for a minute. He laughed, and then burped. He was fucked up. He had never been higher in his entire life. He stood up and staggered. He closed the door and locked it. He rested against it for a minute, and then made his way through the living room. He needed to lay down. He needed to rest for a few hours. He felt like his body was minutes away from giving up on him. He slowly made his way through the hallway. When he got to the end of it, he nodded out for thirty seconds. He woke up when his head fell all the way forward. He wiped his face with his hand. "Damn, I'm fucked up. Bay-bee, where you at?" he asked out loud. He stood there for a minute, then continued to stagger on.

***

Mudman bent Keisha over the couch. She popped back on her legs and spread them. Mudman rubbed all over her juicy ass. He smacked it and watched it jiggle. "Damn, shawty, yo' li'l ass so thick. I can't stay away from dis right hurr. Ain't no way I can do dat." He slid back into her and leaned down.

Keisha arched her back and met him. He sucked on her neck and rocked in and out of her. Her walls clutched him like a fist. "Oooh. Oooh. Oooh. Mudman. You so wrong. You so wrong, baby."

Mudman stood straight up and grabbed her hips. He rubbed in between her ass crack, and proceeded to pound her out all over again, fucking her hard and fast.

Keisha couldn't be quiet any longer. She screamed, and bounced back on him, taking all that he could give her and even surprising herself. "Yes. Yes. Yes. Oooh. Shit, yes!" she hollered. She slammed back into him and held his hip so he would remain planted as deeply into her as possible.

Mudman felt her heat and couldn't help releasing his seed. He jerked and came back to back. "Damn, Keisha. Fuck," he uttered, twitching on top of her, feeling her shake underneath him.

***

Prentice stood in the middle of the stairwell with his mouth dropped wide open. He watched the scene unfold. He couldn't believe the betrayal. The treachery of it all. His high was completely blown. He shook his head and tiptoed back up the stairs.

Chapter 8

It had been a month since Prentice and Mudman had formed their crew of savages, and already it had blossomed into a group of fifteen cold-hearted men with nothing but money, murder, and revenge on their minds. Mudman stood at the top of the totem pole. He was followed by Prentice, and Prentice was followed by Figgady. Out of all the young heartless animals, Figgady was the most cold-hearted, and Mudman took a liking to him right away.

Two weeks after they had formed their Cartel, Figgady had pulled up on him one Sunday afternoon as he was leaving Prentice's crib on his way to get breakfast for the whole house. Once again, the night prior, Prentice had nodded out after getting fucked up on Sinaloa and Lean. As soon as he passed out, Keisha and Mudman were at each other like horny teenagers. Mudman fucked her in the pantry up against a shelf full of flour and sugar. One of the bags of sugar had fallen on the floor and busted all around their feet, and they ignored it while their quickie took place. As soon as it was over, Keisha showered first, followed by Mudman, who fell asleep on the couch with a sinister smile on his face. What he didn't know was that Prentice stood over him for a full hour while he slept with two .40 Glocks in his hands, debating on taking his life and then Keisha's. He knew that he would kill both of them when the time was right. He was just waiting on the right moment - that moment being whatever he had going on in his head.

The next morning, after Mudman took their orders, he left the house, and that's when Figgady pulled up on him. It was five o'clock in the morning. "Say, old head, let a nigga rap wit' you fo' a minute," the young assassin said as he pulled up in a blacked-out Tahoe truck.

Mudman turned around and walked over to the truck. He had his hand on the handle of his .45 and was ready to blow Figgady's shit back if it came down to that. "What's good, li'l homie?"

Figgady had a Tech .9 on his lap and a Kevlar vest across his chest. Half of his face was covered with a blue bandanna. His eyes were bucked and glossy. "A ma'fucka wanna show you somethin'. Come fuck wit' me for a minute." Figgady was so high that he couldn't help grinding his teeth together. He reached into his console and popped a handful of Jolly Ranchers.

Mudman looked both ways and pulled on the door handle. Although he knew Figgady was crazy, his heart didn't pump no Kool-Aid. He proclaimed himself to be the craziest nigga in Baton Rouge, Louisiana. He jumped in the truck and slammed the door. "A'ight, let's roll out."

Figgady eased the truck away from the curb. He nodded his head to a track by Lil Bibby. "Dese my niggas right hurr. Ma'fuckas from Chicago, just like me." He slung his dreads out of his face and mugged the traffic through his windshield.

Mudman didn't fuck wit' shit that wasn't born and bred out of Baton Rouge. He didn't even like New Orleans niggas. He was a savage swamp nigga at heart. He felt that New Orleans niggas were more city than swamp. They were softer. He would blow one back like a blunt any day if they said any different. "Fuck you up dis early for fuckin' wit' me? Specially listening to this Chicago shit. Ma'fucka, dis the south. It's Baton Rouge or nothing round dis bitch." He flipped off the music and mugged Figgady.

He nodded and sucked his teeth. "I wanna show you somethin." He kept cruising and adjusted the Tech on his lap. They rolled in complete silence for twenty minutes.

Figgady pulled into an alley and drove down it. He pulled into an abandoned garage and threw his truck in park. "Come on, Round." He opened the door and hopped out of the whip.

Mudman opened the door and adjusted his guns. The garage had a musty smell to it. The stench was enough to make his stomach turn. He ignored it as best he could. He pulled his hood over his head and followed Figgady out of the garage. They got to the back door of the house, and instead of Figgady knocking, he pushed the door in with his shoulder. It opened. "Come on, big homie, I got some shit you gon' wanna see. I did dis all on my own too." He waved him into the house.

Mudman waited for a second and looked both ways. He could hear the birds chirping in the backyard in one of the trees. A car rolled past the front of the house and continued on its path down the street. The air smelled like it was going to rain. All seemed calm to him. He wondered what the fuck it was that Figgady had to show him. He stepped into the house and closed the door behind him. He looked it over for a lock and saw that the one attached to the door had been busted off.

Figgady lurched up the stairs one at a time. He checked over his shoulder to see how close Mudman was to him, and then kept on going on his way. When he came to the back door that opened to the residence on the downstairs of the duplex style home, he pushed it inward and waited for Mudman to walk past him. "Welcome to dat real shit."

Mudman looked him up and down and clutched the handle of his pistol. He stepped past Figgady and into the lower level of the duplex. The back door led into a kitchen. The first thing Mudman saw as soon as he stepped into the kitchen was a Mexican man sitting in a chair at a dinner table. Though he was sitting, his body was slumped forward. A puddle of blood formed around his chair. On the top of the table were small red brain fragments. Mudman looked over to Figgady.

Figgady smiled, showing off his golds. "Bitch-ass nigga didn't wanna talk. You know how dat shit go. Come on." He stepped over a puddle of blood and cruised to the back of the house.

Mudman followed once again, surveying the area as he went along. In the hallway was another Mexican male. He laid on his face with six big holes in his back. There was so much blood in the hallway that the carpet felt like Mudman was walking on a soaking wet mat. The house began to smell real foul, as if the bodies were already decomposing, Mudman guessed both bodies had already released their full bowels.

Figgady led him to a pair of stairs. He took them and wound up on the second floor of the duplex. Once there, he took a short hallway all the way to the end and pushed in the door. He stepped into the room and cracked his knuckles. "I'ma show you how I get down, big bruh."

Mudman peeked his head into the room and saw that there was a round table. Around the table were three men and one female. All four were duct taped to their chairs, with their mouths taped as well. There was three bricks of Sinaloa on the table, and a pile of money that came to thirty thousand dollars. Mudman wondered why the hell Figgady would leave that kind of work and money on a table. Did he not know that his mission could have been compromised at any time?

Figgady pulled back the closet door and pulled a bag containing what he called his hitta's kit from it. He slammed the bag on the table and looked over at Mudman. "You say we hunting these Cartel niggas, right?"

Mudman looked over the captives and nodded his head. "Yeah."

"Well, that dope right there is dat Sinaloa Tar. That shit official like a referee. If dey got bricks of dat shit here, dat mean dat dey connected to dem ma'fuckas back in Mexico. Prentice told me about da hit they put on y'all. Dese ma'fuckas gotta know something. The streets talk, and dey yelling dat dese ma'fuckas that hustle out dis trap report back to Mexico City, and da Sinaloas back dere. We finna see." Figgady knelt down and pulled a big screwdriver from his bag. He grabbed one of the Mexican men by his shoulders and scooted his chair all the way back until the chair was against the wall. He squatted in front of him and mugged his red face. "Say, muthafucka, you remember me?" He pulled his blue bandana down and revealed his face to him. Off of the strength of that, Mudman already knew that the rules of the jack boy game said that Figgady had to kill the man because he had seen his face.

The man mugged Figgady and remained still. He closed his eyes. Figgady ripped the tape from his mouth. He thought that it may have been the reason he hadn't responded. "You heard what the fuck I asked you?"

The man opened his eyes and sneered at him. "You are a dead man. You just don't know it yet." He hawked a loogey and spit it directly into Figgady's face. It landed in his eye and dripped off of his chin.

Figgady stood up and pulled his bandanna all the way from around his neck. He wiped away the man's spit and tucked his bandanna into his jacket pocket. "Dat's how you wanna play dis shit? A'ight den."

The Mexican man clenched his teeth. "You dead, muthafucka. You're a dead man walking. You and that nigger behind you. Both of you are - "

He felt Figgady slam the screwdriver into his face at full speed. The metal penetrated his sinus and pierced his brain. He felt something explode inside of him, and then his blood was rushing out of his nose. Before he could swallow, Figgady was stabbing him again, this time in the left eye. It popped. It was the worst pain he had ever felt in his entire life. He screamed like a bitch. Figgady slapped the tape back over his mouth and went crazy stabbing him back to back, over and over, until his head swelled up and his life left him

Mudman looked on with a grin. He watched the man fall forward, lifeless. This was definitely up his alley. "You feel better?" he asked, almost jokingly.

Figgady mugged him. He stood, breathing heavy. He wiped his mouth with the back of his hand before grabbing the next man. He ripped the tape from his mouth. "Who da fuck y'all work for?" He ripped the tape from his mouth.

The Mexican glared at him. "Fuck you!" he spit.

Figgady was ready for it his time. He moved just in time. The spit landed on his shoulder, a big yellow glob of it.

The Mexican mugged Mudman. "I feel sorry for you, Mudman. When they get ahold of you, you'll pray for death."

Figgady grabbed him by the throat and plowed him with forty stabs before his life departed from him.

"Dis yo' plan? You finna keep asking dese ma'fuckas if dey know anythang, knowing damn well dat dey ain't gon' say shit?" Mudman asked, feeling a chill go down his spine because the man had known his name.

Figgady stood there with his left arm covered in blood from his stabbing. "Dese ma'fuckas know something. How else you gon' find out who put that hit on you and da homie? Dis da only way."

Mudman surveyed the last two. "Grab dat bitch. She already crying and shit. She knows something. I know she don't wanna wind up like da rest of dese ma'fuckas."

Figgady grabbed her and slung her chair to the floor. He ripped the tape off and knelt over her. "Bitch, who y'all work for? Who put da hit on my homeboys?"

"Please! Please! I don't got nothing to do with anything. I'm innocent. Please don't kill me. I'm only visiting!" she yelled.

Figgady grabbed her throat and squeezed as hard as he could. "Which cartel do your people work for? Tell me bitch? Tell me right now?" He squeezed harder and harder.

She shook and more tears came out of her eyes. "Akk, akk! Please!" she croaked.

Figgady let her go. "Speak, bitch."

She turned on her side, and spit. "Okay. Okay." More spitting. "The Sinaloas."

Figgady turned around and looked up to Mudman. "I knew it."

Mudman looked down at the woman. "How did dude's bitch ass know my name?"

She lowered her eyelids. "You're Mudman?"

He pulled his hood back. "Yeah, bitch, the one and muthafuckin' only."

"You're a problem. You hit the wrong hustlers and fucked over the wrong people. You cost the cartel a nice amount of Baton Rouge money. Because of you, the quota ain't being met here. Well, you and another dude. Both of you have to go, and soon, according to word throughout the tops of the cartel."

The last Mexican man that was bound began screaming into his tape. He shook in his chair and tried his best to break free of his binds. He wanted to kill the woman, his sister, for talking. Her snitching could mean death for their entire bloodline.

Mudman mugged him and looked back down at her. "So, you saying they want me dead. It's not a matter of if they will kill you, it's only a matter of when, and how sadistic."

She smiled at this.

That sent another chill down Mudman's spine. "A'ight, bitch. Dis yo' lucky day. I'm finna let you go."

"What?" Figgady snapped.

Mudman stood up and pressed his barrel to the remaining man's forehead and pulled the trigger twice. The back of his head blew against the wall before he slumped over and died seconds after.

"Noooo!" the woman screamed.

Mudman stood before the woman and grabbed her by her throat. "You tell dem ma'fuckas to come get me. Tell dem dat Mudman said he ain't running. Tell dem dat I said Baton Rouge, Louisiana is mine, and I ain't going nowhere. Dat if dey want war, den let's get it. You hear me?"

She nodded. "Yeah, I hear you." Her eyes lowered again. Mudman was a fool, she thought. He would be dead by sundown, she was sure of that.

Mudman released her from her binds and stood back. "Get up, and go tell dem."

She rubbed her wrists and watched him the whole time. When she got to her feet, she looked down on her brother that had been slain. A lone tear dropped from her eye. She mugged Mudman again and shook her head. She hated him. She hoped they tortured and then murdered him.

"Okay, I'll go deliver your message."

She turned away from Mudman and Figgady stepped into her path. He pressed both barrels of his .45s to her cheeks and pulled the triggers at the same time, blowing her face off. All she saw was a bright light, and she felt a burning pain before everything went black.

Figgady looked over to Mudman. "Nigga, you tripping. Let's get the fuck up out of here."

They grabbed all of the Sinaloa Tar and money before leaving in haste.

Hood Rich

Chapter 9

"Dang, Mudman, you did all of dis fa me?" Keisha asked, looking around the penthouse suite. The room was all white, from the blankets on the bed to the drapes covering the windows. The entire room was littered with red and white rose petals. Keisha already had a Chanel bag under in her hand. Mudman had bought her a brand new red and black skirt dress, with matching Christian Louboutin heels.

Mudman looked around the room and smiled. He hadn't lifted a finger. He'd simply paid the hotel staff at the W to make sure that his suite looked as good as it did. He stepped in front of Keisha and slid his arms around her waist. "Man, shawty, I told you dat you deserve da best. Ma'fuckas out hurr trapping in dese streets, getting all dis money. Who else I'ma spend it on?" he asked. He kissed her on the forehead and allowed for his lips to rest there.

Keisha shuddered in his arms. She hugged his waist and held him. After he broke the kiss, she stood back, and looked up at him. "Rome, why are you doing dis?"

Rome was Mudman's government name. Nobody called him that other than his mother. He felt some type of way about Keisha using it, but he didn't want to ruin their good mood. "I just like you, shawty. You're a good girl. All dese niggas out hurr ain't doing nothing but praising dese yella hoes. Well, I see beauty in you, and dis is a ma'fucka praising you." He kissed her lips softly at first, the top, and then the bottom one, before sucking all over them.

Keisha engaged. She melted into his embrace and became lost. She rubbed all over his massive back. She could feel his muscles protruding everywhere that she touched.

She broke the kiss and wiped her lips a little. "Damn, Mudman." She plopped on the bed and lowered her head. "You're fuckin' me up. What am I supposed to do about your cousin? Where does Prentice fit into all of dis?"

Mudman locked the door to the suite and placed his guns on the dresser. He pulled his shirt over his head and shrugged his shoulders. "Look, I don't know. I told you before that I ain't tryna break up y'all happy home. I ain't tryna take you away from him, but I want a piece of you too. It's as simple as dat."

"But it's all dese other females out there, Rome. You got a nice bag on you now. You're a handsome dark-skinned Kammron. Dem hoes'll eat yo' ass up. You don't need to pursue me. I'm hitched already. Damn." She rubbed her temples.

Mudman slid beside her and wrapped his arm around her shoulders. "I'm riding fa you, shawty. I'll smoke a nigga or a bitch fa you. I'm addicted to dat shit you got between dem thighs right dere." He slid his hand between her legs and patted her pussy. "Fuck dem other hoes, dey ain't got shit on you. It's as simple as dat."

Keisha allowed his words to soak in for a second. On the one hand, she appreciated him for putting her above so many other women. It felt good to be desired and courted. It made her feel like a woman. It had been so long since Prentice had expressed any desire in her. She felt ugly to him. She felt worn out. Mudman made her feel so wanted. That was a weakness for any woman who was not getting that desired effect at home from her own woman, or man. It would be so easily for her to fall for Mudman, but then what would happen? He and Prentice would always be cousins. She would always be the woman that came between them, and she would always be the one that betrayed

Prentice, a man that she had loved ever since she was ten years old. She wondered why life had to be so hard and confusing.

She stood up and looked around. The room seemed to close in on her. "Mudman, dis ain't right, li'l daddy. I can't keep shitting on my man like dis. I mean, I appreciate everythang that you doing for me, but the price is one I ain't willing to pay. I'm sorry." She hugged herself and turned her back to him.

Mudman sat on the bed for a second and then rose from it. He slid behind Keisha and pulled her back to his chest, kissing her neck. He could smell her Prada perfume that he'd bought. She felt soft in his arms. "Shawty, I'm down to fight fa you. I ain't about to let you leave me behind and cut me off for nobody. You my ma'fuckin' Eve, I can feel it."

"No, Mudman, don't say dat. You don't even know what you're talking about. You've never read the Bible in your life."

He held her tighter. "I have, when I was in there. I know what it means to call a woman yo' Eve. It means that she was meant for you, just like you really are for me. You can't fight dis shit, boo." He sucked her neck and ground into her ass.

Keisha could feel the length of his pipe elongate against her ass cheeks. It felt thick and good. She shivered. "Mudman, you starting to fuck wit' my emotions li'l daddy. You're leaving pieces of you in my brain. I can't handle dis shit. I swear I can't." She turned around and looked into his eyes.

Mudman rested his forehead against her smaller one. "I just wanna make you happy, Keisha. I wanna spoil yo' li'l ass, and make you feel like a Queen. You already know I ain't got nobody dat I love outside of my mama, and shawty struggling on dat shit. I need to love somebody. A ma'fucka can't be all killa, all da time." He kissed her lips again and picked her up.

Keisha wrapped her thighs around him and placed her cheek against his. "I'm falling in love with you Mudman. I'm getting confused. Instead of dreaming about Prentice, I'm starting to dream about you, and it's killing me. You gotta release me, baby, please. This could never end well."

Mudman shook his head. "Nall, shawty. Fuck dat. I can never do dat. You're my baby. I gotta have you." He carried her to the dresser and set her on top of it. He lowered his head and tongued her down while he unbuttoned the Christian Dior top that he'd purchased for her. "You can still have Cuz. I ain't gon' never break da up."

Keisha laid her head back and allowed for him to kiss, and suck all over her neck. She felt her temperature rising. She heard the words coming out of his mouth and knew that she wasn't that type of female. She wasn't the type to run back and forth between multiple men. She had that faithful bone deep in her core. She still couldn't understand how Mudman had managed to penetrate, and break that bone, but she felt horrible that it had happened.

***

Prentice listened to both Mudman and Keisha's entire conversation. Keisha, being negligent, had speed dialed him on the phone when she'd sat on the bed. He chopped up the Sinaloa on the table in front of him and sprinkled a nice amount on to his spoon before fixing it up and getting it ready to go into his syringe. He couldn't help but to think murderous thoughts. He'd never thought that Keisha would betray him. He could never see Mudman crossing him in the way that he was. It made his blood boil and his hatred intensify. "I'm killing both of dem ma'fuckas. Watch. Dey gon' do me like dis? Yeah, a'ight." He nodded his head and sucked up the drug into his syringe. He found a vein quickly, right in the center of his bicep. A minute later the drug was injected, and he was feeling breezy. He laid his head back with his temper beating as he heard Keisha screaming and moaning at the top of her lungs.

***

Mudman laid back in the king-sized bed while Keisha rode him, holding on to the headboard backwards. He watched her ass jiggle and shake as she bounced up and down, riding him like Roxy Reynolds, his favorite porn star. He smacked that juicy ass. "Get that shit, baby. Fuck! Get it!" He humped upward and fucked deeper into her hole.

Keisha screamed, "Aw shit! Shit. Mudman, you turning me out. Uh! Yes! Fuck, you turning me out!" She wiggled her hips in a circular motion, and then she was grinding into him, and rotating her hips all over again.

Mudman closed his eyes and sucked on his bottom lip. *Ain't nobody got that killa pussy like Keisha. Nobody,* he reiterated in his mind.

***

Prentice nodded in and out and jerked awake when he heard Keisha scream as loud as she could. He jumped up and punched a hole in the wall. "Punk-ass bitch!" he snarled and began to pace back and forth. He stopped and looked down at the phone. Next, Mudman was groaning. He imagined he was cumming. There was more squeaking from the bedsprings for another two minutes, and then it was quiet. Prentice grabbed his phone and turned it off.

***

Three hours later, Mudman wrapped his arms around Keisha's waist while the boat cruised out into the water amidst the starry sky. They were on a short one hour cruise and were on their way back to shore after having a nice meal followed by soft jazz music, where they danced and enjoyed each other's company. There was a light breeze coming off of the water that felt good to the both of them.

Keisha felt Mudman kissing her neck. She smiled and rubbed his arm. "I had a good time, Rome. I don't think I'ma be able to look Prentice in his eyes, but nevertheless, I had a good time."

Mudman scanned their surroundings. All along the deck were couples hugged up, staring out into the water. He sized them up for a threat assessment, and figured they were harmless. He eased back into his lovey dovey mode with Keisha. "Dat's all da matter to me." He stepped forward and made sure that his piece was on her ass. She was fitting the Chanel skirt dress so well. She had her hair all done up, looking like a Goddess straight from Africa. In his opinion, Mudman, didn't think that there was a finer woman than the dark-skinned ones.

Keisha allowed for him to kiss her neck some more. It felt so tantalizing. She got goosebumps. "Mudman, can I ask you a question?" She looked out into the water and imagined the boat crashing into an iceberg and sinking. She wondered of Mudman would be able to save her, or if they would both drown. She couldn't swim to save her life, so she hoped she wouldn't have to save his swoll ass.

"Shawty, you already know you can. What's good?"

"How do you do it?" she asked.

"Do what?"

She sighed. "Rome, how do you look Prentice in the eye every day knowing that you're sleeping around with me? Doesn't it make you feel some type of way?"

Mudman wanted to say "hell n'all". That he didn't give a fuck how another nigga felt. He didn't give a fuck about manly emotions period. He didn't think niggas were supposed to have them anyway. But he could tell that Keisha was struggling with something. He had to make it seem like they were on the same level for the most part. "Shawty, I feel horrible 'bout what we doing every day, but a ma'fucka can't help how he feel about you. You somethin' special, and I ain't willing to back away from somebody that I care about much as I do you."

Keisha's knees got weak. For as long as she'd known Mudman, she always thought him to be emotionless. She couldn't see him caring about anybody, especially not her. To hear him express his feelings for her felt so good that she grew instantly weak. "Do you really thank dat I'm worth all dis drama that's about to come our way if he ever finds out about da two of us? You know he gon' snap. That boy just as crazy as you is."

Mudman chuckled at that. "You thank so?"

"Hell yeah. I done been wit' him when he dome murked something before. He can be heartless too."

Mudman kissed her neck. "Dat shit ever come out, you just blame it on me. I'll take full responsibility for everythang that we got going on, you got my word on dat, a'ight?"

"I'm woman enough to stand on my own two feet and admit what I've done wrong. I'll never cower like dat. Do you wanna know something else Mudman? And please don't overreact to me telling you dis."

The wind blew her curls Two of them stuck to her chocolate forehead and made her look so sexy. Her almond eyes popped in the nighttime. "Speak yo' mind, shawty."

"I'm falling in love wit' you, Mudman. I think I need to sit down wit' Prentice and tell him how I'm feeling. What you think?"

Mudman, held her for a moment in silence. "Nall, shawty, we don't even know where we going wit' shit yet. Let's just chill for a moment. When bruh get back from New Orleans tomorrow I'ma holler at him, if it I feels right." Mudman didn't have any intentions of doing anything of the like. He cared about Keisha, but he didn't know to what extent. He felt that what they were doing was good enough for him for the moment. After all, he didn't want to take her away from his cousin.

"Okay, Mudman, I'ma let you run da show. But before you holler at him, can we all sit down together and get an understanding? I just feel like that will be more mature."

He kissed the back of her neck. "Yeah, boo, dat sounds cool. Now relax and let me enjoy the rest of dis time I got wit' yo' fine ass tonight. Tomorrow, we back to da basics."

"Okay, and maybe sometime tonight you can tell me what me letting you know that I'm falling in love wit' you means to you." She grunted and rolled her eyes, though he couldn't see it.

"Bet those," was his only response.

Chapter 10

Prentice lowered himself inside of the Chevy Caprice Classic. He wiggled his fingers inside the black leather gloves and watched as Junkie jumped out of the black-on-black Lincoln Navigator. He had two swoll bodyguards behind him. They wore leather jackets and jeans that were way too tight for Prentice's liking. He felt the Percocets drip down the back of his nostrils into his throat. He was gone off of two grams of Sinaloa, and could barely keep his eyes open, but oddly enough, he was on point and ready for action.

Mudman eyed the trio through the window. He grabbed the suitcase full of newspaper from the back seat and placed it on his lap. "Mane, you ready to handle dis hurr bidness?"

Prentice wanted to turn to his side and knock Mudman's head off. Every time he heard his voice now he imagined the sound of him moaning, along with Keisha. His flesh crawled just being so near him. "I was born ready, homeboy."

Prentice opened the door and stepped out of the car. He gazed around the place they were. The refrigerator warehouse was located in the back of another glass warehouse. The alley was huge. To the right of them were four semi-trucks that transported the refrigerators and air conditioners. It smelled like gasoline in the air. A short distance off were train tracks and a highway. Both men could hear the cars whooshing by on the freeway.

Mudman stepped out of the car, high off of Percocets and Mollie. He was laser focused and in the mood to kill something. His pupils were dilated, and for some reason, he felt angry. He could sense the tension between himself and Prentice, and he wanted to address it, but he thought there was a better time to do it. Real killas never missed all of the signs of another man's change in behaviors or patterns. Something was most definitely bothering Prentice, and this picked at Mudman.

They walked side by side until they got to the back steps of the warehouses, where both of Junkie's men met them. Mudman walked up and past them. He beat on the door to the warehouse. "Say, Junkie, mane, I know you seen a ma'fucka pull up."

One of the bodyguards stepped up and beside Mudman. "Say, potna, Junkie in dere waiting on y'all. You Mudman, right?"

Mudman looked him up and down. "Why da fuck you asking me all dese questions, homie? Dat ma'fucka just seen me roll up. He should be out hurr, not you."

The swoll security guard laughed and rubbed his bald chin. "Before y'all go in dere and holler at the boss, a ma'fucka gotta pat y'all down. Rules are rules." He acted like he was getting ready to touch Mudman.

Mudman grabbed him by his neck with blazing speed. He slammed him into the door and busted him through it. The metal door swung inwards, scaring the shit out of Junkie. He jumped back with one of the Mach .90s in his hands. The table was loaded up with an array of them. Mudman came from under his shirt and slammed the barrel of his .44 Desert Eagle to the security guard's temple and cocked the hammer. "Bitch-ass nigga, if you ever in yo' life think you about to touch me, I'll smoke yo' whole family. Do I make myself clear?"

The security guard, caught off-guard, nodded. He was stuck. There was nothing else he could really do. "A'ight, man, damn."

Mudman searched him and retrieved his gun. He put it on his waist and slung him to the ground. "Turn yo' punk ass over."

The man turned over in a hurry. He held his hands above his head. "Junkie, call dis nigga off, mane. Tell dis ma'fucka I was just doing what you told me to do," he said with a cracking voice.

Junkie slammed a clip into the Mach .90. "Let him go, Mudman. Da boy only doing what I told him to do," Junkie said. He didn't know whether to raise his gun or to keep it at bay on his side.

The second security guard acted like he wanted to reach for his weapon. As soon as he reached under his shirt, Prentice upped his .9 and smacked his across the face with it, splitting his forehead. "Fuck you thank dis is, homeboy?"

The second security guard fell to his knees. He reached under his shirt and upped his Glock. He cocked it and aimed.

Mudman caught his movements from the corner of his eyes. He aimed and busted his gat three quick times, rushing toward the man. "Fuck nigga!" The gun jumped in his hand and spit shell casings into the air. His bullets zipped across the warehouse and landed into the side of the man's head, shredding it.

Prentice's eyes were bucked wide open. He raised his .9 and popped the first security guard four times, and then stood back. The man shook on the pavement, leaking. Then he took another gun off of his waist and raised both guns at Junkie. "Nigga, you already know what time it is."

Junkie wasn't going quietly. He squeezed his trigger on the Mach .90. The bullets zipped across the warehouse and cut up the floor and the metal garage door. The noise echoed loudly in the small warehouse. Both Mudman and

Prentice dove to the floor. Junkie took off running toward the back of the warehouse.

Mudman was on his ass busting. Boo-ah! Boo-ah! More running. He watched Junkie disappear into the shadows, then he heard a loud kick of a door. Junkie had kicked open the fire escape and took off running outside to his truck. When he got in front of it, he sprayed the door.

Mudman ran back a little bit. He waited until the shooting stopped before running out the door. When he got outside, he saw Junkie just pulling off. The tires of his truck kicked up rocks. Then he was storming away. Mudman ran behind the truck for a short distance and stopped to shoot. His first bullet busted out the back window. The second lodged itself into the front windshield and cracked it.

Junkie stepped on the gas and got away. He made a hard turn at the end of the alley and was sideswiped by Figgady's black van. Figgady had his homie behind the wheel. He pulled the side door open and let his automatic shotgun ride, aiming at Junkie behind the steering wheel. Boo-wah! Boo-wah! Boo-wah!

Junkie swerved, and there was the sound of crunching metal. He pulled off into the street just as Figgady busted another round. The bullet crashed through his truck side window and knocked the right side of his face off. It landed all over the dashboard.

Figgady watched the truck slowly roll into the street before it came to a halt against the curb. He hopped out of the van and ran over to check the condition of Junkie. Junkie lay up against the steering wheel with blood spilling all over the floor mats. Figgady placed the barrel of his Draco to the back of his head and pulled the trigger. When he walked back to the van, he'd left Junkie with nothing but a neck. He'd even taken the time to snatch the Mach .90 off of his lap.

***

Mudman looked over the Mach .90s an hour later inside of his Trap. He had them laid across the wooden table. They looked so pretty to him, all shiny and steel. They even smelled brand new. He smiled and nodded his head at Prentice. "Ma'fuckas finna change the game wit' dese bitches right hurr."

Prentice picked one up, and once again, he felt like taking Mudman's life. "Yeah, mane, you already know what dis finna be about right hurr." He looked through the scope and zoomed in to a spot on the brick wall of the basement.

Figgady raised his head from tooting two Percocet sixties. He was feeling breezy, sipping on a bottle with pure pink Mollie inside of it. "Mane, dat ma'fucka thought he was finna make a clean getaway. Guess he didn't know who he was fucking wit'. Dis Cartel Killaz right hurr, mane. Ma'fucka finna get dat shit tatted right across my belly." He smiled and ran his tongue across his teeth.

Mudman handed him a Mach .90. "Dis ours right hurr, li'l homies, and dis one right hurr for ya mans that pulled that move wit' you. He ain't allowed in the secrecy of the Trap, but you handle dat shit wit' him. Feel me?"

Figgady nodded and stood up. He shook up with Mudman. "Love, fool. I'm finna be out dis bitch. I got bidness to take care of."

Mudman shook up and stepped to the side. He wasn't with that hugging shit. He knew that Figgady had a habit of showing mad love to him and Prentice with a half hug. "A'ight, li'l nigga. Good looking on dat shit too."

"You know it. Figgady gon' always come through for the fellas. Know dat." Figgady grabbed Prentice's hand and shook up with him as well. He took the time out to give him a half hug. "Love, big homie. I'ma fuck wit' you niggas in the morning."

Prentice returned his love and handed him his weapons. "Don't forget dese.

Figgady grabbed his guns. "Never that. I need dese ma'fuckas just to breathe."

***

Mudman waited until Figgady left and turned to Prentice. "Nigga, what's good wit' you?" He took one of the Mach .90s and sat on the couch with it.

Prentice mugged him from across the room. "Fuck is you talking about?" Prentice turned his back to Mudman and picked up a choppa He slipped a clip into the handle and cocked it back.

Mudman watched him closely. "Nigga, you got somethin' on yo' chest?"

Prentice shook his head. "Nope, I'm kosher, my nigga. Why you asking me some shit like dis? Fuck going on inside of yo' heart?"

Mudman stood up from the couch. "Da last couple days you been acting real funny, nigga. You acting like one of dem fuck niggas in da street. I don't know what yo' problem is, but you already know I don't do dat emotional shit. If you got a problem wit' me, spit dat shit out."

Prentice waved him off. He had visions of unleashing the whole clip into Mudman and calling it a night. He couldn't believe how he and Keisha could betray him. His heart hurt like it was being stabbed repeatedly. "You bugging, Cuz. I ain't got nothin but love for you. Good looking on smoking dat nigga for me tonight. I sho' froze. Had you not been there, he would have hit my ass up. I'm sho' of dat." Prentice needed to defer the conversation. It was pure killa 101. Never allow your target to know that you are hunting them, or what is going on inside of your brain. He knew that Mudman was a maniac. If he'd let on that he knew about him and Keisha and that he was feeling some type of way about it, Mudman would have killed him for sure. Prentice already had his mind made up. He needed to use Mudman for one major score, and then he would murder his ass in cold blood and keep the spoils of their lick. He just needed for them to hit a lick that would give him enough money that would help him leave Baton Rouge behind forever. He had family in Oakland. His people were plugged over there. If he could get to Oakland with a big enough bag of cash, he could start over and become a king in his own right. Yeah, he had to keep Mudman close for the moment.

Mudman cleared the space between them and stepped into Prentice's face. "I smell something foul wit' you, homeboy. I don't like how I'm feeling. I think we got something dat need to be settled."

Prentice looked into his eyes and stepped forward until their noses was touching. "Nigga, I said ain't nothing wrong wit' me. Now I don't know what you searching for, but I'm good. You need to get yo' monkey ass out of my face. Dis ain't dat tonight, potna, dat's on my mama."

Mudman looked into his eyes. He could feel the Angel of Death waiting in the corner of the room. A cold chill went down his spine. "I'ma ask you one mo' time. Are we good, or do you got something on yo' chest you wanna holla at me about?"

Prentice looked into his eyes. "Bruh, it's late. Dat dope got yo' ass bugging. I'm getting hotter and hotter. If you don't get yo' ass out my face, we 'bout to tear dis basement up. Now move, nigga." Prentice bumped him out of the way, took half of the choppas that were left, and slid them into his duffel bag. "Get some sleep hurr tonight. I'm finna go home and fuck my bitch all over that house." He tossed the strap of the duffel bag over his shoulder and made his way out of the basement.

Mudman stood there in silence for a long time after Prentice had left. There was something about his last statement that got to him. He felt a wave of unexplainable jealousy because of it. When he imagined Prentice climbing between Keisha's thighs, for some reason, it made him sick on the stomach. A part of him wanted to show up unannounced. He wanted to break up what they were about to do. He slumped on to the couch, stuck. He didn't know what to do.

Chapter 11

Keisha raised her head from under the covers. She could have sworn she heard a noise. She reached and switched on the lamp that was on the side of the bed. Then she listened more carefully. Sure enough, she heard a door opening and closing. There were footsteps coming down the hallway. She looked to the right of the bed and saw that it was vacant. She became worried. She slipped out of the bed and rushed to the dresser. She knelt down and pulled the bottom drawer out. Reached inside of it and grabbed the .380 that Prentice had given her for her twenty first birthday. She cocked it back and aimed it at the door. "Who da fuck in house?" she hollered.

Prentice stopped in his tracks. He wondered who in the hell Keisha was talking to. The hallway was dark as sin. He felt along the wall until he got outside of the bedroom door. He grabbed the knob. "Shawty, who da fuck you hollering at?" he asked, opening the door.

Keisha waited until she was able to make him out and sighed in relief. "Holy fuck, Prentice. You can't be sneaking up in da house like dat dere. You already know how bad my anxiety is." She lowered the gun and sat on the bed.

Prentice eased into the room and closed the door. "Fuck you talking 'bout? What? You want a ma'fucka to ask you permission before I come in my own damn house or somethin?" He frowned.

Keisha rubbed her right temple. "Nall, I ain't saying shit like dat. Earlier doe, I saw two black Benzes parked in the front of da house. Dey wasn't moving or doing shit either. After a while, dey just pulled off. It was strange too. Plus, dey had dem Texas plates on 'em. We don't know nobody in Texas; at least, I don't."

Prentice grew worried for a minute. He sat beside her. She could smell his body odor, and it made her cringe. "You didn't see what color the dudes were inside of it?"

She shook her head. "Nall, dey had dem mirror-tinted windows. For all I know, dey could have been females." Now that Prentice appeared worried, it only made her anxiety worse. "Why, you expecting somebody to be doing something to you from Texas?"

Prentice couldn't help but to think about the Sinaloa Cartel and how he and Mudman had been picking off all of their local Baton Rouge workers one by one. He knew that eventually they would seek their revenge. It was only a matter of time. But he also knew that if he let on that there was an impending threat, Keisha would panic. He couldn't afford that right now. The Percocets and heroin had him feeling like a champion. He needed some of Keisha. It had been so long since he'd had some of her. "Shawty, ain't no telling who dat was, but it wasn't nobody looking for me." He stood up and pulled off of his shirt.

Keisha took the .380 and put it back into the bottom drawer of the dresser. Then she slid into the bed, pulled the covers over her body, and directed the fan so that it blew directly on her. Prentice's body odor had already lit up the room.

Seeing Keisha bend over had set Prentice's libido on fire. Keisha's short nightgown had raised up far enough to show off the fact that she wasn't wearing panties. He made out the lips of her sex. He settled beside her and rubbed her thighs through the blanket. "Damn, baby, you can calm down. Daddy hear to protect you now."

Keisha froze. She hoped that he didn't have on his mind what she think he did? "Prentice, I'm tired, honey, I gotta get up early in the morning. I got an interview at Verizon Wireless," she said, scooting away from him just a bit.

Prentice ignored her and began to pull the cover down. "Dat's all fine and dandy. You go on and go to sleep. I'ma do what I need to do anyway," he promised.

Keisha held on to the cover. She could smell his musty underarms. She could only imagine what the rest of him smelled like. She figured that if they were going to do anything, that he would have to get into the shower, but she had been down this road with him before, and she knew where it ended. "Baby, what's going on with you, are you feeling some type of way?" she asked in her most sultry voice.

Prentice yanked the blankets off and exposed her sexy chocolate legs. "Hell yeah. I don't give a fuck what you talking 'bout. You finna give me some of this cat tonight, shawty, or I'm finna take dis shit," he threatened.

Keisha trembled. She felt him trail his hand up her inner thigh. Before he could touch her pussy, she jumped out of the bed. "Look, Prentice, I don't feel like it tonight. Plus, you still ain't washed yo' ass. Baby, can't you see how you're lighting this room up?"

Prentice grew angry. "Bitch!" He slammed his fist down on the bed. "Don't you be talking 'bout how I smell. You ain't never had a problem wit' it before, now all of da sudden you do? Fuck dat!" He jumped from the bed and slammed her against the wall. He held her by her shoulders and flared his nostrils angrily.

Keisha closed her eyes. She couldn't stand to look into his face. His breath smelled rank. As close as she was, she could not only smell his underarm, but his privates as well. It was sad to her, yet still, she loved him. "Prentice, baby, I don't mean to offend you. I swear to God I love you, and

I want to desire you, but in order for me to do so, you're going to have to get into the shower, please. Matter fact, let's do it together."

Prentice flung her to the floor and kicked her in the ribs. She flipped on to her back. "Bitch, how da fuck you saying you love me? You don't love me," he snapped.

Keisha curled into a ball and stayed that way for a few moments. Tears fell down her cheeks. "Why are you doing this, Prentice?"

He grabbed her by her lace front and pulled her to her feet. "Bitch, I oughta kill you." He grabbed her around the neck and squeezed.

Keisha allowed for him to choke her for a split second, and then she brought her knee forward as hard as she could. She felt it land in his lap. The next thing she knew he was on his knees, wincing in pain. She punched him in the jaw as hard as she could.

Prentice felt the intense stinging in his groin, and then the hit to his jaw pushed him over the edge. He growled and fell against the bed. "Bitch, I'm finna kill you," he swore.

Keisha rushed him swinging haymakers. Four of them landed into his face, and then she was on top of him. She grabbed his face and bit into it. "I'm tired of you treating me like shit. I'm tired of you putting your hands on me. You don't own me. You don't rule me. Ahhhhhhh!" she screamed, really fuckin' him up.

Prentice had no other choice other than to accept the assault. He could feel his lip and face bleeding. Something in him snapped. He hollered and rose to his feet. As soon as he was there, he began to pummel Keisha with blow after blow. He knocked her out with the third punch. She landed on the floor. He straddled her, raining down blows.

"Bitch, I told you." Punch after punch. Tears ran down his eyes. He kept on punching, over, and over.

Mudman rushed into the room and flung him off of her. Prentice crashed into the dresser and knocked it completely over. Before he could get to his feet, Mudman rushed him and lifted him up in the air, then slammed him as hard as he could on his back, knocking the wind out of Prentice.

Prentice rolled over and struggled to catch his breath. "You saving dat bitch," he gasped and struggled to breathe.

Mudman stood with his chest heaving up and down. "Nigga, what the fuck is wrong wit' you? Dis girl been by yo' side since da beginning. Now you doing dis shit?"

Prentice crawled around on the floor and used the wall to stand up. His back felt like it had been broken. "Fuck y'all. Both of you muthafuckas." He grabbed his shirt off of the bed and made his way to the hallway.

Mudman rushed to Keisha's side. Her face was fucked up. He kissed her lips. "Aw shit, baby. What the fuck have you done, Prentice? What have you done?" He looked back into her battered face. A tear dropped from his eye.

Keisha opened her eyes and tried to talk, but only blood came out. She felt excruciating pain on nearly every part of her body. She couldn't believe that Prentice had done this to her. "Help me, Rome. Help me, please."

Mudman, lifted her up. He wrapped a sheet around her body and rushed toward the front of the house. "Just hold on, baby. He got you. Just keep fighting."

As soon as he opened the front door to the house, three black Mercedes Benz cars pulled up to the curb and seven masked Mexican cartel members jumped out of them. They were armed with handguns. They ran toward the house.

Prentice saw the impending attack and ran back toward the house. He was more than halfway to his truck. "Shit, hold that door!"

Mudman hurried backwards and fell with Keisha in his arms. She rolled off of him and wound up on her back again. He picked her up just as the shooting started and took off running toward the back of the house.

Prentice dove into the hallway that led inside of the house. Bullets chopped at the wall in front of him, leaving big holes inside of them. He stopped, turned around, and got to shooting back at the cartel.

Their bullets came in flurries. The windows to the house exploded. The walls burst with big holes inside of them and drywall smoke filled the house. All three occupants coughed from the big cloud.

Mudman lowered Keisha into the tub of the bathroom and kissed her forehead. "Shawty, stay yo' ass right thurr. Don't get up." He knew that she had a strong chance of surviving in the tub because the bullets had a hard time penetrating the surface of the tub's basin. "Promise me that you won't move!" he snapped.

Keisha's lips had swollen up. They felt like boxing gloves on her face. "I promise."

Mudman crouched down and entered into the hallway while bullets zipped down from the shooters outside. He closed the bathroom door and rushed to the basement. He was met by Prentice. Prentice was already slamming a hunnit round clip into his Mach .90. Mudman grabbed one out of the duffel bag and did the same. The house felt like it was shaking in an earthquake. As soon as his machine gun was loaded, he hit it out the back door and jumped over the neighbor's fence. He needed to get the ups on his attackers. In order to do so, he stood a better chance of bucking at them from the neighbor's yard. It would surely catch them off-guard, he figured. Prentice ran and jumped the other neighbor's fence. He was on the same thing.

Mudman got to the front first. He watched the masked men chop at Prentice and Keisha's home with no regard for the life inside. This infuriated him. He knelt in the gangway and peered at them through the scope. There was no doubt in his mind that they had to be cartel. They wore black ski masks with white dots all over them. The license plates on their vehicles read that they were from Texas. Mudman knew that Texas was a Sinaloa stronghold. He aimed and waited until the plus sign settled on the first target's head, then he pulled the trigger. Bocka-bocka-bocka!

"Awww!" The man's head split down the sides before he fell backward.

Prentice picked a target and slayed him with precision. The big Mach .90 jumped in his hand. Its bullets flew into the attackers, chopping them down with ease. Prentice clenched his teeth and kept right on busting back to back. When another man caught five to the neck, he smiled.

The Sinaloas began to retreat for their cars. They busted back at the pair before jumping into their whips and storming away. Mudman continued to chop at their cars. He busted their windows and fucked up the paint on their foreign whips. He ran and stood over the four dead that laid in front of the houses and finished them with face shots, no mercy style. "Prentice, get rid of dese bodies, mane, I gotta get shawty to the hospital."

Figgady and five members from his crew rolled up and jumped out of a black Chevy Astro Van with choppas in their hands. Figgady looked around. "What da fuck going on?"

"Don't stress 'bout dat right now. Help me get these bodies in that van before dem people come," Prentice hollered.

"Dem ma'fuckas ain't coming Cross Da Tracks, mane. Dey know betta."

Cross Da Tracks was the deadliest hood inside of south Baton Rouge. It was located on Garfield and Roosevelt. All of the killas Cross Da Tracks didn't have any problem fanning Twelve down. They held no regard for authority. "Throw dem ma'fuckas inside, mane. Y'all two go to dem corners and make sure that don't nobody come down this block until we get this hurr figured out," Figgady ordered. He watched his men scurry from the van to do what they were told.

Prentice gave him a half of a hug. "I don't know what I would do without you, li'l homie."

Though these were the words that came out of his mouth, all he could think about was what he'd done to Keisha. He regretted every second of it, and the love that he held inside for her caused him to have remorse that he didn't even know he possessed.

Figgady nodded. "Don't even mention it. Now help me clean up dis blood and shit as best we can."

Chapter 12

Keisha opened her eyes two days later. When they came into focus, she turned her head to see an empty chair in the hospital room. The sight caused her heart to drop. She felt sick. She was expecting that somebody would be there for her. She couldn't imagine who she'd want to be there, but she just hoped that it would have been somebody. She tried to lift her right arm, and for the first time, she noticed that she was hooked up to an I.V. Suddenly her eye sockets began to hurt, along with her jaw. She felt the faint pain in her ribs, and then the attack was coming back to her full fledge. She started to panic. She took a deep breath, but that did nothing to stop her blood pressure from sky rocketing. Her monitor began to go crazy.

Mudman had been staring out of the hospital window. He'd been so lost in his thoughts he'd not even noticed that Keisha had come to. "Aw shit."

The dark-skinned nurse rushed into the room and over to Keisha. "Baby, are you okay?" she asked, resting her hand on the top of Keisha's forehead and looking over her vitals on the monitor's screen.

Mudman came to her side. "Keisha, baby, what the fuck? You okay?"

Keisha perked up. So, he was here, she thought. That made her instantly emotional. "I'm good, Rome. I'm just freaking out."

Two more nurses ran into the room. "I'm sorry, sir, but you're going to have to step into the hallway until we get her under control," the older of the pack relayed.

"I ain't going no muthafuckin' whurr. Dis my shawty right hurr. Y'all betta fall back," Mudman warned. He had a .40 Glock on him, and he didn't have any gripes about using it.

"Sir, but - " the older nurse started. She was seconds away from calling security.

"Please let him stay," Keisha begged. "I need him here."

The older nurse looked her over with sympathy, and then she looked to her colleagues. "Baby, I don't mind him staying here, but I just have to ask you one question before we allow that?"

Keisha tried her best to sit up straight. She felt the pain in her ribs and exhaled loudly. She settled back on the big hospital pillows. "Go ahead, ma'am."

The older nurse stepped forward and leaned into Keisha's face. She looked back at a frustrated Mudman and back down to Keisha again. "Baby, he's not the one that did this to you, is he?"

"Man, hell n'all!" Mudman snapped. "Y'all in dis bitch tripping fa real now."

"No, ma'am. He's the one that rescued me from my attacker. If it wasn't for him, there is a potential that I could be dead right now."

The older nurse felt sympathetic. "Oh my." She checked over Keisha's vitals and saw that they had gotten better. She rested her hand on her forehead again. "Okay, baby, well, we'll leave you two alone. Just hit that there button over there if you have any trouble. Okay?"

Keisha nodded. "Yes, thank you."

The older nurse smiled and ushered the rest of her colleagues out of the room after taking a glance back at Mudman. The sight of him gave her chills. She wondered how many people she'd worked on at the hospital had life threatening injuries that he'd caused. He looked like a cold-hearted murderer to her. She shivered once again before closing the door behind her and her staff.

Mudman walked over and locked the door. Then he came and stood beside Keisha. She reached out for him. He hugged her into his arms. "Keisha, damn, shawty. You already know dat had I been thurr earlier, I would have never allowed for dis shit to happen to you. I should fuck Prentice up for dis."

Keisha hugged him tighter. "It's just bad karma, Rome. We been doing what we been doing behind his back, and it's just the universe's way of getting me back. I deserve this."

Mudman scrunched his face. He peeled her off of him and looked down at her. "No, da fuck you don't, Keisha. Dat nigga, or no nigga at all, ain't got no reason into be putting their hands on you, period."

"But I deserved it, Rome. Eventually he gon' find out about us, and he gon' wind up killing me anyway. I might as well get ready for dat."

Now Mudman was really steaming. He slipped on to the bed with her and pulled her into his arms. She winced from the pain in her ribs but fought through it. Mudman wrapped her into his arms and kissed the side of her forehead. "Keisha, dat's my ma'fuckin' cousin, shawty. Dat nigga Prentice is my blood." He was quiet for a moment. He held her more firmly. "But you wanna know somethin'?"

Keisha looked up to him. "What's dat, Rome?"

Mudman took a deep breath and exhaled. "When I came thurr and seen him doing what da fuck he was doing to you, shawty, I wanted to smoke his ass right thurr. Shid, to be honest, when he told me that he was going home to fuck you all over dat house, it's the reason I came over dere to begin with. I think I was on some sucka shit. Fact, I know I was. I think I care about you a whole lot, shawty."

Keisha was stunned. She stared at him with her eyes wide open. Tears sailed down her cheeks, and she hated herself for being so emotional. She tried to summon her strength of toughness, but she couldn't help that his words had struck a chord within her emotional safe. "So, what are you saying, Rome? Are you saying that you really wanna be with me?"

Mudman sighed. "I don't know what I'm saying, other den I care 'bout you, and you make me feel shit I don't like feeling. I don't like being reminded that I got a heart. I done did too much wrong to get a heart now. My shit gotta stay black as midnight, but I can't help when I think 'bout you, I get dis weird shit going on inside of me."

Keisha smiled, and then laughed. She felt so happy, and she couldn't understand why. She had hated Mudman for as long as she'd known him. She couldn't deny the fact that she found him attractive, but his personality and disrespectful ways had always thrown her off. She felt that he was so cold and callous. She couldn't see why any woman would waste their time with him, and she for damn sure couldn't see any one of them falling in love with him like she had to admit that she was doing. "Rome, I love you."

Mudman cringed. He tensed up and slowly slipped from their embrace. He stood on the side of her bed and shook his head. "Keisha, I don't think I got dat love shit in me, shawty. I ain't tell you all of dat to try and game you or somethin'. I was just telling you what was on my mind."

Keisha forced herself to sit up. She reached out for his hands. When she had them inside of hers, she pulled him closer to her. "Rome, look at me."

Mudman looked everywhere else's but her face. He couldn't stand to see her injuries. She had two black eyes. Her jaw looked swollen. Whenever he imagined how Prentice looked beating her senseless, he grew angry. He hated himself for putting his own hands on her back in the day. He wished that things were different, but most of all, he wished that he had never crossed those lines with her.

"Rome, I love you, and it's okay if you don't love me as well. Everybody knows that you are a muthafuckin' thug. They know that you 'bout dat life. You can be hard for them, but you can show me that you care about me when we are together. Every killa has a weak spot. Why can't I be yours?"

Mudman yanked his hands away. "Because you my cousin's bitch. It's gon' always be dat way. You been wit' Prentice since y'all was in the fourth grade, mane. Dat's a long-ass time to be with anybody."

Keisha forced herself up to her knees. She adjusted her I.V.s in her hand accordingly. "Rome, bring yo' ass here. Now!"

Mudman was pacing. He stopped and mugged her. "Why da fuck you keep calling me by my government?"

"Get over here, Rome," she said sternly.

Mudman stayed planted for a moment, and then he made his way in front of her. "What up?"

She grabbed his jacket and pulled him closer to her until she had her nose pressed against his. "You don't think I'm smart enough to know what I had with Prentice, and how much history we have together?"

"I ain't say dat."

"You're his cousin. Y'all have been thick as thieves ever since we been in grade school. I know that I am about to create a war. I don't want to cause dis drama, but at the same time, I love you, Mudman. I love you, and I have fallen out of love with Prentice. It just don't feel the same between us anymore. But it's not just about the feeling of dat. Da fact of da matter is dat you got my heart, and I can't stop thinking 'bout you either. Prentice would have killed me had you not stepped in. You somethin like my hero. Every girl wants to be with her hero." She smiled and kissed his cheek on both sides. When she felt him remain still, she moved her head backward and looked him over, feeling a bit insecure. "What, you ain't feeling me no mo' or somethin'?"

Mudman didn't know what to say. He didn't like feeling all sappy and emotional. He figured that those types of things weren't inside of him, and he hated Keisha for proving otherwise. Her presence, her scent, her warmth, her voice, all of it was enough to drive him out of his mind, and he hated that fact. "Keisha, I just thank we should be smart until we figure out what you gon' do wit' Prentice. You already know dat I'm out hurr in dese streets. Any day could be my last. It'd be real selfish of me to allow you to fall in love wit' me, and den I wind up losing my life before this hurr week is out. Fuck type of man would that make me?"

Keisha balled his jacket into her right hand. She yanked him closer to her. "Nigga, dis shit right hurr ain't just 'bout you. It's 'bout us. Now nigga, I know damn well you feeling some type of way 'bout me, otherwise you wouldn't be the only one in dis hospital right now concerned 'bout my well-being. You ain't gotta be tough wit' me, Rome, damn."

"Keisha, it ain't about me being tough."

"Den tell me you love me. Just keep dat shit real right now," she challenged.

Mudman felt like he had to shit. His stomach did a somersault. He had never uttered those words to anyone outside of his mother and sister Miami since he'd been alive. He didn't even think he could for them, because he had not said them in so long. "Keisha, what you gon' do about Prentice?"

"Damn Prentice right now. Mane, go 'head and tell me dat you love me. I need to hurr dat shit because I feel so weak. Please, Rome." She squeezed tears out of her eyes.

Mudman felt a lump form inside of his throat. He swallowed it as best he could and looked into her eyes. "Keisha, why are you crying, baby?"

She shook her head and wiped her tears away. "Cuz it shouldn't be so hard for you to tell me how you really feel about me. Why are you so stubborn?" She covered her face with her hands.

Mudman felt horrible, and he hated himself for feeling that way and for allowing the small emotions that he had to get caught up into Keisha so much so that her feelings made him feel some type of way. But more than anything else, he didn't like seeing her hurting. "Keisha, baby."

She waved him off. "Nall, Mudman, just forget it."

He reached out for her. "Bring yo' ass over hurr now, stop playin' wit' me."

Keisha mugged him. "Damn, can you be a li'l nicer?"

"Nall. Now come hurr."

She frowned and came to him. "What?"

He took a hold of her wrists and looked into her eyes. "Listen to me. I just want you to know that, I really do care about you. Outside of my mother and my sister, you're the only person that I honestly love in dis world. I hate seeing you hurting, shawty. I hate not having been there to protect you from the very beginning. I promise to never let you reach harm again, as long as I can prevent it. A ma'fucka gon' feel dis steel if dey fuck wit' my baby, dat's how that's gon go right durr."

Keisha was smiling hard. Tough-ass Mudman had expressed his feelings to her, unabashedly. She felt privileged, and a whole lot of special. She didn't know the right words she should have said to him, so instead of saying anything, she pulled him to her herself and they began to make out like horny newlyweds. She didn't even let the pain in her jaws, or the pain that resonated all over her body affect her. All that mattered was that he'd finally said it.

They broke apart after two straight minutes of moaning and kissing. "So, what are you going to do about Prentice? We can't keep going behind his back like kids."

Keisha agreed. "I know, but what do you suggest? Should we talk to him together, or separate?"

Mudman shrugged his shoulders. "I don't really know. Let's take a few days, get you back healthy, and den we'll figure it out from den on."

Keisha nodded. "Okay, baby, dat sounds good to me." She pulled him to her. "We gotta get the fuck out of Baton Rouge, Rome. Dem cartel boys gon' wind up killing one of us. I keep having dese nightmares and thangs. Just somethin telling me dat something bad gon' wind up happening if we stick around hurr." She held the side of his handsome, dark-skinned face.

"Yeah, I thank I agree wit' you. Let me finish up what I started down hurr, get my bag up a bit more, and we can bounce."

Keisha screeched, and grabbed him to her again. "Rome, are you serious?"

He laughed. "Yeah, Baton Rouge burned up. It's time I left dis hurr city behind."

Chapter 13

A month later, and the Cartel Killaz had been in one war after the next. It seemed to Mudman that everybody in Baton Rouge was coming up with fully automatic weapons. Their shootouts had been very close calls. So far, they had only managed to have a few casualties. Now that most of the armed dope boys, and jack boys in Baton Rouge knew who they were, whenever they saw members of the Cartel Killaz, they were arming them out on sight, and Mudman and his crew of savages stayed ready for that gunplay. It was a deadly game of war, but one that the Cartel Killaz were forced to be a part of.

Mudman screwed in the red light bulb in the basement and pulled his metal chair away from the table before sitting in it and pushing it back to the head of the table. All around the table were bloodthirsty Cartel Killaz. Some were nodding in and out, gone off of the best Sinaloa Tar in the state. Others were gone off of pills and pure codeine. The table had platters of tar and mini bowls of pills. The men slid them up and down the table to one another and took what they wanted to.

Prentice sat at the far end of the table, fresh off of shooting a gram of ninety-eight percent pure tar into his veins. He nodded and leaned to his right. A slight trace of drool seeped out of the corner of his mouth. Just when it looked like he was about to fall over he would jerk upward and catch himself.

Figgady tooted a thick line of Percocets and chased his drip with a double cup of pure codeine. His eyes were low. The lids were heavy as anvils. He slurred his speech. "Mane, it's 'bout time we hit somethin' major." He nodded out.

Prentice was just coming from a short nod. His eyes were red as a pool ball. "I agree. Dese niggas out here playing wit' dem fullys. We gotta step our game up and get some shit to protect our chest, mane. It's only a matter a time before a nigga puts some heat in one of our asses."

Mudman tooted two hefty lines of pink Mollie. He held his head back and kept trying to swallow his spit. His ears started to ring. The Mollie was ninety-eight percent pure. It looked like pink lemonade rocks before he'd crushed them up. "Li'l homie say he got a big score. Ma'fuckas need to hear shawty out, mane."

Figgady nodded. He laid with his head on the back of the chair. After nodding like this for two full minutes with nobody talking, he came to. "Y'all know my baby mama a Dominican bitch from up there in Boston. She stayed in Lawrence out that way." He nodded and dozed off.

The entire basement was full of snoring for five straight. Arms fell to sides. Mouths were wide open. Some of them were scratching themselves, and each man had a fully automatic weapon on his lap, or on the table in front of him. Mudman sat at the head of the table watching them all. He didn't know what to say. He was fighting the nod himself.

Figgady came back to and slammed his hand on the table. Everybody woke up. They began rubbing their faces. All were irritated at the sudden noise. "Y'all ma'fuckas need to listen to what I'm saying."

Mudman agreed. "Go on 'head, li'l buddy."

"I'm a big nigga, but look, like I was saying... My baby mother is a Dominican bitch. All of her uncles and cousins are fresh from the Dominican Republic, and they working with that top notch dog food straight from the island." Dog food was another slang terminology for heroin.

Prentice got his works ready. He was already imagining shooting the Sinaloa into his veins as he cooked it in his metal top. "A'ight, so what you getting at?"

Figgady nodded but kept talking. "I got the drop on one of their safe houses out there in Lawrence. She was there last week, and she took a bunch of pictures and shit for me. Check dis shit our fight hurr, potna." Figgady pulled his phone from his inside coat pocket. He slid it across the table to Prentice.

Prentice flipped through the pictures. He saw one with a table full of kilos. It looked to be no less than eighty bricks stacked up. Another picture showed a bunch of money. Prentice surmised that it had to be every bit of a million dollars. Another pictured showed a room full of artillery. This one made him nervous. He slid the phone all the way down the table, and into Mudman's hands.

Mudman picked the phone up and looked over the same pictures that Prentice did. "How da fuck she get all dese flicks?"

Figgady opened his eyes and forced himself to sit up. "Dem her people. Dey love her, but she love me. Dat's what dat is right thurr. My bitch gon' always do what I say."

Mudman scanned the pictures again. "Let's talk strengths and weaknesses." Mudman knew that if the Dominicans were holding like this, that they had to have a list of both.

Figgady took a nice gulp from his double cup. He felt the codeine sting his throat. "Strengths: they'll kill yo' ass dead if we make any wrong move. We gotta go in dis ma'fucka expecting to lose a few of us. Ain't no such thang as all of us walking out of dis bitch alive, I'ma tell you dat shit right now."

Mudman kept flipping through the pictures. "Fuck dese bitch-ass niggas. What's dey weaknesses?"

"Dese ma'fuckas shoot that shit all day long, which means they got a problem wit' nodding. The second weakness is my bitch. She knows how this particular trap house works. She says her uncle Stevo loads it up every other Wednesday because the Dominican Cartel he works for come pick all dat shit up in a semi-truck and moves the contents up and down I-95. Boston is just a drop off and a post used to mass distribute on the east coast."

Mudman raised an eyebrow. "You been treating dat girl right?"

"I'm Fat Figgady, it's that bitch's job to treat me right. Dis part of the criteria for her being wit' me. Like Moneybagg say, dat bitch wit' whatever I'm wit', know dat," Figgady said. The Mollie and the Lean had him feeling himself like masturbation.

Prentice closed his eyes. "We fuck around go out dere fuckin' wit dem Dominicans, we'll get our asses smoked like Newports."

Mudman shook his head. "Not if we handle dis bidness right. All I need is some time to prepare. We can hit dis safe house?" He was already imagining what the money could do for him and Keisha. Now that she was a few months along, Mudman was thinking about leaving Baton Rouge behind. His enemy list was growing daily. He didn't want to bring a child into the world under those conditions. Yeah, he had to do right by Keisha. He owed her that.

"A'ight den, let me set some shit in motion wit' my bitch. I'ma report back to you personally, Mudman," Figgady assured him.

Prentice didn't like that. He felt that since he'd brought Figgady into the fold that he should have addressed him about everything first. He disliked how most of the members of their crew looked up to Mudman as if he was the supreme leader of their crew, but in his opinion, they were equal. Mudman wasn't calling shots over him. He would never allow for that to happen.

Figgady stood up and staggered on his feet. He shook up with Mudman and nodded at Prentice. He knew that they had their work cut out for them. He needed to get into the best possible graces that he could with his baby mother, Chela.

"A'ight, fellas, dat means we got a mission to get ready for. We gon' let Figgady handle his bidness, and as soon as he get back to me with the specifics, I'ma set a plan in place so we can buss this move. We need them choppas and dat work." Mudman said.

"Yeah, and more than dat, we need that money before they hand that shit off to whoever it's supposed to be going to," Figgady spoke up. "I'm ready to have a li'l cushion in my finances." He was already imagining what it would be like to have about a hundred and fifty thousand dollars tucked away. He needed that security, not just for himself, but for his daughter and baby mother as well.

Prentice stood up. "Den we all know what we gotta do. As da heads, me and Mudman gon' figure dis lick out and make sure dat we go in dere da right way," Prentice said, looking down the table at Mudman.

Mudman curled his upper lip and ignored him. "Meeting adjourned, fellas."

Slowly but surely, the men started to gather their things, and disburse. It took about twenty minutes for everybody to clear out? When it was all said and done, the only two left remaining were Mudman and Prentice. They remained sitting at the table, Mudman at the head, and Prentice down at the foot.

Mudman looked down the table and drummed his fingers on the table. He mugged Prentice from a distance. "What's good wit' you, Cuz?"

Prentice pulled his nose and sat back in his chair. He sucked his teeth, then leaned all the way forward with his elbows resting on the table. He clasped his fingers. "Nigga, you thank you running dis hurr thang, don't you?"

Mudman continued to mug him. "I'm a born leader. A muthafuckin' boss. I don't follow no muthafuckin' man. You niggas gon' follow me, so you gotdamn right. I KNOW I'm running dis cartel."

Prentice knew it. He hated Mudman's ego. He hated how the man always acted like he had to run everything. He felt that Mudman thought he was better than him. He was looking for a reason to set some shit up anyway after what had taken place with Keisha about a month ago. "Well, let me tell you dis right now. You might be running dem other sendoff niggas, but you don't run me, Mudman. I run me. Long as you know dat, we ain't gon' have no problems."

Mudman eyed him and smiled. He picked up his double cup and downed half of it. The codeine felt good coursing down his throat. The purity caused him to feel the effects right away. "Maybe if you could keep yo' eyes open long enough, you wouldn't have to worry about the young killas dismissing yo' ass and coming to me. We all jack boys at heart. We can tell when a man is weak, or if he is strong, and nigga, all you do is show signs of weakness." Mudman didn't care how the comment affected Prentice. He felt like he needed to hear what he'd just told him.

"Dat's how you really feel?" Prentice asked, standing up.

"Fuck feelings, nigga. Dat's what I observed." Mudman felt the beats of his heart getting faster and faster.

Prentice flipped the table. The ruckus was loud enough that it could be heard outside. "Nigga, I'm tired of yo' shit. First dis bullshit wit' Keisha, now dis?"

Mudman remained seated. He didn't take Prentice seriously. He knew his cousin had that killa shit in him, but he knew who, to play with. Mudman would not hesitate to bust his brain if it came down to it. "Fuck Keisha gotta do wit' anythang?"

Prentice eyed him with hatred. "Nigga, you don't thank I know you fuckin' my bitch? Huh? What, you thank I'm stupid or something?"

Mudman stood up and picked his Draco up off of the floor. He had fifty shots in the magazine of the baby AK47. He hoped he didn't have to use them on his cousin, but he felt that if he had to, he had to. Life would go on. "Dat shit go a li'l beyond fucking. And don't take yo' shortcomings out on me. It is what it is. Dat's my bitch now. Fuck you gon' do?"

Prentice felt like his head was going to explode. He rushed Mudman at full speed and stopped in his tracks when Mudman raised the Kay and pointed the weapon directly at him. "Aw, so dat's what dis is. What, you too chicken to fight me without dese guns?"

"What?" Mudman smacked his lips. "Bitch-ass nigga, what you talking 'bout?"

Prentice picked up his Mach .90 from the floor. "Nigga, we can knuckle up over dis shit hurr. I'd never kill you over no bitch, but you ain't just about to take my bitch from me.

Now if you whoop my ass you can have her, but if I whoop you, den you back the fuck up off my shawty, mane. Bet?"

"Bet those. Nigga, when you wanna do dis?" Mudman could hear the thunder outside. The basement window was slightly opened. They could hear the rain begin to pelt down on the sidewalk.

Keisha had been eavesdropping upstairs with the door opened. She made her way down them. "No, no, no, dis shit ain't 'bout to happen here, mane. Y'all need to stop dis foolishness, and we can figure out dis out like adults."

"Bitch, shut yo' trifling ass up, and go back up dem stairs." Prentice snapped.

She scoffed. "What?"

Mudman closed the distance between them quickly. He stepped into Prentice's face. "Let's handle dis shit like we used to do back in da day, homeboy. Right on Roosevelt and Garfield. Cross da tracks."

Prentice nodded. "You ain't said shit but a word. Winner of dis shit hurr not only gets Keisha, but they stand atop the totem pole all alone of dis hurr Cartel. How dat sound to you?"

Mudman bumped him out of the way. "I ain't finna meet you durr. I'm finna beat you durr." He squeezed past Keisha without saying a word.

That made her feel some type of way. She thought that maybe Mudman was mad at her or something. "Rome, wait."

He ignored her. "Hurry yo' ass up, Prentice. Time is money."

Prentice gathered his things and made his way up the stairs last. When he got to where Keisha was standing, he paused and looked her over. She looked off. She couldn't stand to look him in the eyes. Prentice grunted. "Bitch, after I whoop dis nigga, you finna bring yo' ass home with me, and I'ma fuck da submission back into you. I can't believe you." He bumped her and kept moving up the steps.

Keisha held on firm to the railing. She prayed that Mudman won the fight. She was tired of Prentice, and she couldn't wait to be rid of him. "Please God, let yo' will be done."

Hood Rich

Chapter 14

Lightning flashed across the sky and illuminated the darkness for a split second. The wind howled and blew with an intense draft. The rain fell from the sky harshly. The strong stench of swamp resonated heavy in the air.

Mudman stood in a puddle of mud that came up to his ankles. He could feel the coldness of the wet dirt oozing into his shoes. He clenched and unclenched his fists and stared directly across at an angry Prentice. Keisha sat in Mudman's truck with the windows rolled up. She was shaking worse than a person being naked in a snowstorm.

Prentice stepped forward and splashed the muddy water. Behind him, a train screeched past on its tracks. The noise was almost deafening. They could see the sparks shoot up from the tracks. Prentice slammed his fist into his hand. "Let's handle this bidness, nigga. Fuck is you waiting on?"

Mudman took off his shirt and threw it on top of the hood of his truck. He rolled his head around on his neck and stepped up to Prentice. "What's yo' tap out word?" he asked. Back when they were kids and getting it in with each other, they always had a word they would say to let it be known that they had had enough. For Mudman, it never was uttered, but he took pleasure in making Prentice say it more than once.

Prentice shook his head. "No mercy, nigga." He swung, and rocked Mudman so hard that he knocked him backward. Mudman was dazed as he fell backward.

The next thing he knew, the back of his head was falling into the mud. Portions of it got into his mouth. Prentice clenched his teeth. He could have rushed Mudman, but he didn't want off that easy. He knew Keisha was watching, and he wanted to put on a show for her. He made sure he was good and high off of both heroin and Percocets. It was going to be a while before he felt any pain.

"Get yo' bitch ass up, nigga. We got a lot of work to do."

Figgady pulled the van into the lot and jumped out ten deep with his hittas behind him. Both Mudman and Prentice wanted his presence. They had already said that whoever won the fight would be the official leader of the Cartel Killaz. Though deep in the back of his mind, Figgady wasn't honoring neither man as head. He simply thought it imperative to play his position until he built up the strength and clout and take over the entire organization in his own right. But first, he would watch them dismantle each other, and instead of giving his loyalty to the winners, he was already thinking of giving it to the weaker man because down the road, the weaker man would not only carry a serious grudge against the winner, but the weaker man would be so obsessed with getting revenge that he would be easy to conquer in the short term. Everything that involved the game was like chess. Chess was a game that no real conqueror ever wanted to lose at. Figgady felt that he was meant to be a king, and if he had to climb the backs of Prentice and Mudman to get there, he was all for it.

Prentice looked over and saw the younger Cartel Killaz gathering around to watch the fight. This excited him. "Say Mane, you li'l niggas just in time." He jacked as it began to rain hard.

Mudman made his way to his feet. He spit the dirt out of his mouth and threw his guards up. "A'ight den, Cuz, let's get it." He rushed Prentice. Both men met in the middle of the lot exchanging blows like savages. They were swinging and hitting each other so hard that each blow that landed made the crowd wince. More than once each man fell. The other was crazy enough to step back and allow for the other one to get to his feet, before they were swinging like doped up Boxers again.

Mudman ducked one of Prentice's blows and came up with a right hook that landed on Prentice's jaw. When he hit him, he followed through and dropped him to the muddy water that was now up to their shins.

Prentice fell to one knee. He spit blood into the murky water. The rain was coming down so hard that his shirt was matted to him. He felt dizzy. He closed his eyes to get the world to keep from seeming as if it were spinning.

Mudman danced on his toes. "Fuck is taking you so long? Get yo' ass up."

Prentice stood. He gathered himself. "Good hit. A'ight, let's finish this." He protected his chin and hunted Mudman, rushing him with his head bent low. When he got within striking distance, he gave Mudman two to the body, and one hard uppercut that crashed into his ear. Then he grabbed him by the waist and dumped him in the water.

Both men began to wrestle. Their strength was even. First Prentice would wind up on top before Mudman slung him off. They jumped up and went back to throwing haymakers. Mudman caught one to the nose that busted his shit. Blood spurt everywhere. Prentice's ducked one of his hits, dropped to his knees, and jabbed and punched Mudman as hard as he could in the nuts.

Mudman emitted a groan so loud that he made the alligators in the nearby creek slam their tails into the swamp. The guttural groan sounded like a new Predator to them. Mudman fell on both knees. He was in excruciating pain.

"Hell yeah, nigga, I told you." Prentice cocked back his right leg and kicked Mudman as hard as he could in the chest, knocking him backwards.

Once again, Mudman fell in the muddy water. He laid there for a second, trying his best to catch his breath. The kick to the chest felt like a shotgun slug to him. He was sure that Prentice had broken, or at the very least cracked, a few of his ribs.

"Get yo' ass up, Mudman! Come on, nigga, before I come get you," he threatened.

Mudman stayed still. He could feel the muddy waters going into his ear canal. Rain pelted down on his face. His shoes were flooded. He climbed to his feet and laughed to himself. He was done playing with Prentice's ego. He knew he couldn't fuck wit' his business, and he was about to show him that firsthand. "A'ight, li'l cuz, you got you a few licks in, now let's be serious. Come on."

Prentice furrowed his eyebrows. He was confused and was sure that Mudman must have been trying to play games. Either way, he was dead set on finishing him. He balled his fists as tight as he could and met Mudman back in the middle of the battle ground. Another train came screeching through on the railroad tracks behind them. Prentice swung as hard as he could, trying to knock Mudman's head off.

Mudman blocked it and punched Prentice twice in the face, then swiped his leg, Angola style and hit him with a left hook to drop his ass to one knee. Prentice spit blood into the mud. He glanced up at Mudman's truck where Keisha sat watching from a distance. The lightning flashed across the dark sky and lit up the truck. Sure enough, he could for a split second see that she was watching the entire fight. That vexed him. He stood up.

Mudman was in his mode now. He had been known in Angola State Prison as a knockout king. He waited until Prentice rushed him again with his simple-ass blows. He blocked the first blow, grabbed the back of his head, and head-butted Prentice. While Prentice was falling backward, Mudman jumped and drop kicked him in the chest.

Prentice flew in the air and came crashing down in a big splash of water. He was dazed and confused. Blood rushed out of his nose and over his lips. He struggled to get up. The pain relief from the opiates and heroin was beginning to wear off. His face was stinging. When he made it to his feet, he stood on wobbly knees.

Mudman's dreads were all over his face. He looked like a murderous character in a horror movie. He could smell the fear and pending defeat of Prentice. A part of him wanted things to end there, only because Prentice was his cousin, but then there was the animal part of him that wanted to finish Prentice like the last piece of pizza. Mudman still felt hungry. It was the savage in him.

"Nigga, you quit? Stop dis shit right now, or I'm finna finish you!" he hollered as lightning flashed behind him.

The thunder roared and sounded like a bunch of fireworks going off at once. The rain came down so hard that it felt like hail. Prentice squinted his eyes to see Mudman. His left eye had swollen up, and so had his bottom lip. "Never. nigga. I'm finna kill you. Ahhhh!" He took off running toward Mudman.

Mudman waited until he got within just the right distance, as soon as he was he dropped down, and caught him by the waist. He picked him up in the air and jumped before bringing him down with all of his strength, slamming him in the mud. Prentice's back ricocheted off of the ground and he lost his wind. Mudman straddled him and knocked him out with four quick blows. Prentice lay in the waters asleep.

Mudman stood and looked down on him. The rainwater crashed into his face and head. He grabbed Prentice by the leg and pulled him out of the water. "Y'all put his ass in his truck over durr. Dis shit over wit'."

Figgady nodded at his boys, and they jumped right away to follow Mudman's commands. He walked over to Mudman and gave him a half of hug. "Nigga, you did dat. It's fucked up dat you had to, but you definitely did dat."

Mudman nodded and broke their embrace. "Handle dat bidness wit Chela, mane. We need to make dat trip out dey way so we can get right."

"I'm on it. Just give me a few weeks, and we on dat. Love, fool." Figgady tossed an L at him, and he and his li'l homies jumped in their van and peeled out.

Mudman dried himself off as best as he could before getting inside of his truck. Keisha waited there for him with her hands covering her face. "Shawty, what's wrong wit' you?"

"Dis ain't right, Rome. Y'all shouldn't be doing all of dis shit over me. It's all my fault."

"Shawty, come on wit' all dat shit. What's done is done. Me and dat nigga made a pact. We handled our bidness, and you wit' me now."

Keisha shook her head. "How you know dat he okay? Did you check on him?"

Mudman wanted to snap on her. "Hell n'all. Dat ain't how dis shit s'posed to go."

Keisha opened the passenger's door and rushed into the rain. She ran over to Prentice's truck and pulled open the door. She got inside of it and tended to him right away, cradling his head in her lap. "Prentice, Prentice, please wake up." The state of his face looked horrible. It had swollen so much that he looked damn near unrecognizable. She patted his cheek.

Prentice felt the stinging taps and opened his eyes. "Huh, huh, what the fuck?" he hollered.

Keisha froze up. She started to regret coming over to him. She hoped that he wouldn't kill her, but as long as they had been together, the worst he'd ever done was beaten her up. "Prentice, are you alright?"

He groaned and tried to focus in on what was going on. When he became conscious, he snapped his head backward. "Fuck is you doing here, Keisha?"

"I was worried about you." She tried to touch his face.

He caught her hand and squeezed it until the bones began to crackle. She screamed and he threw her hand away from him. "Bitch, don't you ever in yo' muthafuckin' life touch me again. All dis is your fault. You fucked that nigga behind my back. You betrayed me, and I never thought you ever would."

Keisha felt like shit. "I'm sorry Prentice. I swear I didn't mean for dis to happen. Mudman and I. We're just -"

Prentice turned toward her, reached under his seat, pressed the barrel of his .45 to her forehead, and cocked the hammer. Tears sailed down his cheek, along with muddy water from his scalp. "Keisha get the fuck out of dis truck right now. You broke my heart, and I promise you, as soon as I restore myself, I'ma make you and him reap what y'all sowed. Now get out!"

She opened the passenger's door and rushed out, crying tears of sorrow and pain. How could she have been so stupid? she thought. How could she have cheated on Prentice? Then again, how could she have thought it was a good idea to comfort him after he'd taken such a loss in front of his crew, and her? She ran through the rain, over to Mudman's truck, and got in.

Mudman sat listening to Kevin Gates's new album. He didn't even acknowledge her presence. He simply put his truck in drive and pulled off, though in the back of his mind he hadn't approved of what Keisha had just done. He felt that she still harbored some kind of love and affection for Prentice, and that made him jealous. Jealousy, to Mudman, was a weak emotion, one that he knew he would rid himself of immediately.

Chapter 15

A week later, Prentice was healed up and looking better for the most part. There just a slightly tinge of darkness around his right eye, but it was barely recognizable unless you stared at him for a long time. Prentice had taken a week of baths, two each day, and though his heroin habit was at an all-time high, he was clean and smelling good. He had his waves popping and was fitted in a black and gray Supreme 'fit with the matching retro six Jordans. He pushed his platinum truck down Jefferson Avenue until he pulled up in front of Kayla's crib. As soon as he did, he beeped the horn twice and waited.

Kayla was ready. She kissed her mother on the cheek and rushed out of the door. She stood on the porch of her mother's house and shielded her eyes from the sun. Kayla was 5'5" tall, caramel-skinned with Barbie like-features, natural curly hair, and pretty brown eyes. She was strapped like a top notch stripper. Her body was righteous. Kayla was Keisha's baby sister. She was in her last year of high school, and their mother kept a tight rein on her because she was killing it on the track and field scene. Kayla was Keisha's favorite sibling.

Prentice smiled as he watched her make her way to the car in the tight-fitting Chanel skirt dress. Her thick thighs jiggled with each step. Before she was fully inside of the vehicle his dick was rock hard. He could already imagine some of the things that he was going to do to her either by choice, or by force. Either way, it didn't matter to him.

She slid into the passenger's seat and closed the door. Her perfume permeated through the truck almost immediately. "Hey big bro." She leaned over and gave him a big hug.

Prentice rubbed along the length of her back, then kissed her cheek. "What it do, baby sis?"

She leaned back into her seat. "I'm just so happy to be out dat house. My mama been riding me like crazy. Damn, everybody thanking I'ma do something stupid to trick off my scholarships to run track. Damn, they can give me a li'l mo' credit than that. I ain't did it this far."

Prentice pulled away from the curb. "Well don't worry about me thanking all dat shit thurr, shawty. I believe in you. I know you got dat shit under control. I'm proud of yo' li'l fine ass too."

Kayla blushed. Anytime Prentice gave her a compliment, it made her feel some type of way. Although she looked up to him as her older brother, she couldn't ignore the fact that he was a man, and her mother and family kept her shielded from the male species altogether. As it stood, she went to an all-girls school, and everywhere she went, her mother was by her side. If not her mother, then it was Keisha, though lately Keisha had backed off. She seemed to have a list of her own problems to manage.

"Thank you, Prentice. Where is my sister at?" Keisha hadn't really gotten into contact with her for nearly a week. She would respond very briefly to Keisha's texts, and that was unlike her. Keisha wondered if she was okay.

"She working. That girl always working," he lied. He didn't know where Keisha was, and he didn't give a fuck either.

He looked down and saw the way Kayla's skirt was raised on her thick thighs, and it caused him to shudder. He was willing to bet that nobody had gotten ahold of that young pussy yet. It was like he could smell her virginity in the air, and he wanted it. "Besides, li'l sis, it's like I told you on the phone, dis day is all about you and me. I'm proud of you, and I wanna spend some cash on you. Now can I do all dat, or you want me to take you back home?"

Kayla shook her head so hard that she felt like she was getting a migraine. "Uh uh. We good. I wanna roll wit' you den."

"You remember the stipulation though, right?" he asked, holding his hand out as he came to a stop at a Stop sign.

Kayla reached into her purse and pulled out her cell phone. She held the power button and turned it off before handing it to Prentice. "Here you go."

Prentice took the phone and slipped it into his pocket. "A'ight, we good to go now. Sit back. You see dis right hurr" He pulled a twenty thousand dollar knot of hundreds out of his pocket and handed it to her.

She held it and looked it over. Her eyes were big as saucers. "Dang, where you get all of dis money from?" She was mesmerized.

Prentice rested his hand on her left thigh and rubbed all over it nonchalantly. Her heat felt good to him. His dick was rock hard. "Dat's just some peanuts that I bought along so I could spoil you. You know you always been like my baby girl. Ain't I always went hard over you?"

Kayla called herself trying to count the money. She didn't even notice that Prentice's hand was all the way under the hem of her shorts. His knuckle brushed against her panties underneath. "Yeah, you have. But you finna spend all of dis on me?"

A car pulled up behind them and blew its horn. Prentice grimaced, pulled his hand from under Kayla's hem, and drove off. "Yeah, I thank you worth it. Yo' sister said I shouldn't, but you my baby. I gotta get you right."

"She said you shouldn't?" Kayla looked offended.

"Yeah, she said you just a baby, and that twenty G's is too much to be spending on a li'l girl," he lied.

"Oh yeah? Well, how much do she think is enough to spend on a li'l girl?" She did air quotes with her fingers.

"A few hunnit."

Kayla smacked her lips. "I ain't no li'l girl no way. I'll be grown soon, and den what she gon' say?"

Prentice shrugged his shoulders. "Don't know and I don't care. Matter fact, I don't even wanna talk about her no more. Dis all about you and me li'l sis. Today, you can have whatever you like, you my li'l lady for da days how does dat sound?"

"Sounds good to me." She rolled the knot of money up and slipped it into her purse.

Prentice peeped her antics. He wasn't about to let her get away with that. He slipped his hand inside of her purse and retrieved his cash. "Nall, we ain't gon' do it like dat. I'ma keep control of dis. It's too many jack boys around, but I got you doe."

Kayla laughed. "I knew you wasn't gon' let me do that, but I still had to try."

"Say, Kayla, can you still dance?" Prentice remembered that Kayla was cold at dancing. It was like she was born with a gift. He thought that her gymnastics classes helped her with that a lot.

"Hell yeah, I can. I'm the best in my school, why?"

Prentice smiled. His gold teeth gleamed in the sun light. "I might let you earn some ones later. Me and you gon' play a li'l game. A'ight?"

She nodded. "Long as I can make some money, it's all good wit' me."

***

Mudman sat on the side of the bed as the obstetrician, placed the wand to Keisha's stomach. She moved it around, until their baby appeared on the monitor. The room was quiet, and then it sounded with the beats of the baby's heart. Mudman felt his stomach drop. He closed in on the monitor and looked it over. "Where it's at?"

The OBGYN came over and pointed to the screen. "See, your child is right here."

Mudman saw the form come into existence before his very eyes. He took a deep breath, and then looked back at Keisha. "Damn, boo."

She looked past him to the monitor. She covered her mouth. She felt happy. She was thankful that Mudman was there to witness of with her. "It's beautiful, Rome. It's our baby, honey. How do you feel?"

He kept his eyes on the screen. "Happy, Keisha. I feel like I gotta get us up out of Baton Rouge before our child gets here. What you thank?"

She nodded. "I think you're right."

***

Prentice held the door open for Kayla as she walked through carrying fifteen bags in her hands. They had been shopping at the mall for four hours straight, and out of the twenty thousand dollars, Kayla had spent every bit of eleven thousand of it. Prentice underestimated her. She came all the way into the house and set the bags on the floor. Then she stepped in front of him and hugged him. "Thank you, big bro. You got me feeling just like a princess."

Hood Rich

Prentice hugged and held her waist. He looked into her pretty brown eyes and kissed her on the cheek. His hands slid down and over her ass. He wanted to cuff the cheeks, but he resisted. "You're welcome, baby girl."

"So, what do we do now? You wanna order a pizza until my sister gets here?" she asked, looking into his eyes.

Prentice slipped from her embrace. He pulled out the knot of cash. "Remember how I was saying I wanted to drop some ones on you while you danced for me?"

She nodded, beginning to get shy. "Yeah."

"Well, fuck dem ones, 'cause I ain't got none in dis knot. How about you dance for me, and whatever bill come up, dat's the bill dat you get. How does dat sound?" He reached into his pocket and pulled out the knot and fanned it out.

Kayla didn't see nothing but hundreds and fifties. "Okay."

Prentice settled in on the couch after turning on some Cardi B. for her to dance to. He held the knot in front of him. "Come on, baby sis."

Kayla felt suddenly shy. "How you want me to dance? I'm a li'l nervous."

He stood up and stepped into her face. "You know how them girls be dancing in a strip club, right?"

She nodded. "Yeah."

"Well, just pretend dat you one of dem. I'ma act like I'm one of da customers. All you gotta do is earn yo' money."

"But you my big brother doe. Dem girls that strip be getting all nasty. I won't feel right doing all dat stuff in front of you."

Prentice se the money on the table and pulled her to him. "Look, I'ma feel weird too, but we just chilling. Fuck

134

it." He gripped her waist and slid his hands down to her big booty. He rubbed all over it and cuffed the cheeks. They felt heavy.

Kayla closed her eyes. Her nipples got super hard. Her li'l coochie grew wet. She became embarrassed. "Okay, bro. I got you."

Prentice grabbed his money and sat on the couch with his dick harder than a brick. Over the years he had watched Kayla blossom from being a li'l skinny girl into a strapped goddess like she was now. The fact that she was so young didn't bother him at all. It only added to his arousal.

Kayla stepped in between his thighs and started to wind to the music. She closed her eyes. She couldn't look into his handsome face. She was too shy. "Like dis?" She turned around and slowly twerked.

Prentice fanned money out at her. "Hell yeah, li'l sis." He watched her big booty shake. The skirt rose and exposed her cheeks. The underside looked darker than her actual skin. This excited him. He fanned more money. "Hold that table and really pop that ass, baby."

She followed his commands. She twerked hard - so hard that her left breast began to make its way out of the dress. She felt it, stopped, and pushed it back in. "Am I doing dis right?"

Prentice stood up and yanked her skirt up her hips. She wore a pair of girly panties. They were white with little hearts all over them. He figured her mother had purchased them for her. They were too small. The material was all in the crack of her big ass. "Hell yeah." Prentice dropped down and kissed her right on the crotch. He could feel the heat of her pussy beating through it.

Kayla moaned. "Oooh, Prentice. What are you doing?"

Prentice pulled her ass back to him and yanked the material to the side. Her bald pussy dropped out. The lips were full of her dew. He separated the folds with his tongue and pushed it into her.

Kayla gripped the table and screamed. "Ohhh, baby. My sister gon' kill you!" she moaned.

Prentice sucked on her gap like an expert. He manipulated her clit and nipped at it with his teeth before sucking it into his lips like a nipple. Kayla hollered and came in minutes. She buckled at the knees. Prentice scooped her up and carried her to his bedroom, where he tossed her on the bed. She landed with her thighs wide open. Her brown cat glistened.

She ran her hand between her thighs and opened her lips. "We can't do this, Prentice. My sister gon' kill both of us." She slipped a finger into her little hole and pulled it out. "Plus, dat's all dat ever been in there." She closed her thighs on her hand.

Prentice took off his shirt and flung it to the floor. "Well, shawty, we' bout to change all dat shit thurr."

Kayla pulled her finger out of her box. "Big bro, how we finna do dat?"

Prentice dropped his pants and laughed. "You finna see."

Chapter 16

Kayla closed her eyes as she felt Prentice sucking on her neck. He had her laid back and was between her thighs with his finger going slowly in and out of her. She arched her back and moaned into his ear. It felt so good, she couldn't deny that fact, but at the same time, she felt so guilty because of who Prentice was to her sister. For as long as she could remember, she had always looked up to him as if he was her older brother. Now, for him to have her laid out in the middle of the bed that she was sure her sister had been in a thousand times before, well, it just felt weird, to say the least.

Prentice, laid her all the way down and unhooked her bra from the front. Her C-cups spilled out. He gripped them and pushed them together, sucking first one erect nipple, and then the other one. "How you like dat?"

In response, Kayla humped up into him and opened her thighs wider. "Mmm, Prentice. Are you sure about dis? What time is my sister getting home?"

Prentice slid the Mollie from under the pillow and slipped it deep into her pussy. He closed the thick lips and held them there. He knew that in less than five minutes, the drug would take effect, and he would be able to fuck Kayla in any way that he wanted to. She was a virgin, but ready. Her body told him everything that he needed to know. "Don't worry 'bout Keisha, baby, tonight it's all about me and you." He opened her lips again to see if the pink Mollie had dissolved. He saw only a sticky trace of it. He fingered her box again to push the rest of it into her body.

Kayla shivered. She opened her thighs wider while his fingers flew in and out of her at full speed. She sucked on her bottom lip. She still couldn't believe that this was happening. The thrill of it all had her feeling so excited and wanton.

Prentice sucked hard on her jewel. His fingers were a blur now. He felt her walls tighten on them before she screamed and started to shake while she came hard. She fell to her back, twitching. She tried to push his hand away, but Prentice would allow no such thing. He lifted his face from her box. It was greasy, and he smelled just like her private places. "You 'bout to give me some of dis young pussy right hurr, shawty.

Kayla continued to shake. She rolled to her side and came to her knees. All of a sudden she felt hot, and then happy. A strong wave of euphoria overcame her. Her eyes lowered and her pupils dilated. Her kitty began to throb out of control. She needed Prentice. She needed him to touch her, or she felt like she would just die. "Touch me, Prentice. Please, big bro."

Prentice smiled. He slid off of the bed, stood up, and came out of his boxers. His piece swung low. "Come hurr, shawty.

Kayla scrambled across the bed. She stopped and sat in front of Prentice. Her eye locked in on his dick. She couldn't believe how big it was. She reached to touch it, then jerked back her hand as if she had been burned. She looked up into his eyes. "Can I touch it?"

His piece jumped up and down. He stepped closer. "You can, but not wit' yo' hands though." He grabbed a handful of her hair and guided her to his crotch. He placed his piece on her lips.

Kayla had never done it before, but she sucked him into her mouth, and her instincts just kicked in. She had watched it done on porno movies a hundred times. She sucked him like a champion. She would gag around it and go right back to sucking like she couldn't get enough of him.

Prentice looked her in the face the whole time. He humped back and forth, making her take him as deep as she could, before she'd gag. The excitement of him fuckin' with Keisha's baby sister did something to him. Within minutes, he was pulling his dick out of her mouth and cumming all over her face and lips.

Kayla felt the hot streams and snuck her hand to her crotch. She slipped her middle finger into her box and worked herself at full speed. It didn't take long before she was cumming. "Ohhh shhhittt!" she screamed.

Prentice pulled her finger out of her and sucked it clean. He turned her around and bent her over the bed. "Bitch, I'm finna grow yo li'l ass right up. You wanna be my li'l hoe, right?"

Kayla shivered. "Yes, bruh. Please. I'm ready." She spaced her knees and played with her clit. The Mollie had fully taken over her. She not only wanted Prentice to fuck her, she needed him to. She rested the side of her face on sheets. She felt his big penis head slipping through her sex lips. It entered into her channel and stopped at the barrier that was protecting her virginity.

"Bitch tell me sho'. Tell me you want me to take dis ma'fucka?" he growled.

"Please take it. Take it, bruh." She opened her lips further for him.

Prentice grabbed her hips and slammed her back to him. He busted through her hymen, and before she could even get used to the feeling, he was fucking her like a complete animal, growling like a monster.

The pain quickly subsided and turned into pleasure for Kayla. She bit into the pillow on the bed and screamed while Prentice fucked her like he hated her. It felt so good that she started to cum, and Kayla was begging him to slow down. But Prentice was having none of that. He dug his fingers into her skin and pounded her out. He took pleasure in watching his piece slide in and out of her fresh pussy.

Kayla balled her hand into a fist and beat it on the bed. Tears rolled down her cheeks because the feeling was so good and intense. The Mollie had her clit extra sensitive. She kept cumming back to back. Every time she came, she fell in love with Prentice. She imagined Keisha walking into the room and catching her getting fucked from the back like she was by Prentice. She imagined what she would say or think, and it made her cum again.

"I'm not no li'l girl! Uhhh fuck! I'm not no li'l girl!" she screamed, backing up into Prentice's lap harder and harder.

Prentice pinned her to the bed and came deep within her womb. He jerked up against her as his seed released itself. Her pussy was tight as a fist and good. He even liked the smell of her. She reminded him of the first time he and Keisha had ever gotten down when they were fifteen. The thought drove him mad. He flipped Kayla over and threw both of her thighs on his shoulders. He lined himself up and slid in hard, then he was banging her out and giving her body all that she could handle for an hour straight. He'd cum in her so much that her lower belly appeared swollen.

***

Two hours later and after their shower, Prentice had Kayla naked, laying on her stomach, with a rolled up hundred dollar bill in her hand. He finished chopping through the Sinaloa Tar and made four thin lines on the mirror. He kissed her neck and set it in front of her. "A'ight, boo, you gon' do it just like I showed you how. Remember, dis gon' be just you and my thang every time we get together. You my baby, and I want you to be turnt like me. You hear me?" He licked into her ear and rubbed her naked ass.

Kayla nodded. "Okay." She placed the hundred dollar bill into her nostril and lowered it to one of the lines. She sniffed as hard as she could and cleared half of it. She stopped and began to cough with her head tilted backward.

Prentice pat her on the back. "Dat's okay, shawty, Dat's normal."

She continued to cough. She felt her body getting numb. Happiness flooded her common sense. Her mouth became dry. Suddenly she felt a desire to finish the line, and to treat the second nostril like Prentice had explained to her. She lowered her head again. She felt like coughing but ignored the feeling. She finished the line and started the second one.

"Dat's my baby right dere." He opened her thighs and snuck his face between them, then he was giving her the best head of her young life, driving her absolutely crazy.

Prentice had one goal in mind, and that was to turn her completely out. That was all that mattered to him. He would show Keisha, and in due time, he would show Mudman as well.

***

Mudman finished setting the table and stopped to light the two candles that were in the center of it. Once they were lit, he turned off the lights in the dining room. "A'ight, Keisha, bring yo li'l sexy ass on. Everythang ready for you."

Keisha hung up the phone with her mother and felt worried. Kimmy was saying that her daughter hadn't been home in nearly five hours, and that she wasn't answering her phone. She told Keisha, that it was completely unlike Kayla to do such a thing. She heard Mudman call out to her a second time.

"Here I come, baby, let me wash my hands real fast." She grabbed her phone and sent Kayla a quick text letting her know that she was worried about her and that she needed for her to hit her up right away. Keisha wondered what had gotten into her sixteen-year-old sister. She was usually a good girl. She prayed that everything was all right.

Mudman stood tall as Keisha entered into the living room five minutes later, rocking the Fendi dress that he'd bought her. She was barefoot. Her freshly pedicured toes looked good even in the candlelight. He held her chair out for her and pushed it in after she took a seat.

Keisha looked around at the presentation, and to say that she was amazed was an understatement. "Damn, baby, you did all of dis for me?"

Mudman was kinda proud of himself. He took a seat across from her after popping the bottle of Moët. "Yeah, after seeing our baby inside of you, I just wanted you to know how happy I truly am, and how crazy I am about yo' li'l sexy ass. You brang me joy, shawty, straight up. He grabbed her glass and began to pour the champagne into it.

Keisha looked him over like he was crazy. "Uh, what are you doing?"

"Shid, this bottle cost a whole ass G, I'm tryna buss it down wit' you. Why, what's da problem?"

Keisha crossed her arms and sat there for a moment. She couldn't believe how simple Mudman could be at times. She stood up and rubbed her belly. "Did you forget that we got a lot going on all up and through here?" she asked, smiling, looking all sexy and shit.

Mudman grimaced. "Fuck, I'm tripping, baby. Dat's my fault right thurr. Good save."

"Right. I'm just saying." She sat back down and covered her lap with a big napkin. She looked over the plate of food: T-bone steak, a baked potato, corn on the cob, and a chocolate cake. A meal fit for a true queen. "Damn, baby, this really does look good though. Thank you."

"Shawty, I appreciate you."

Keisha grabbed his hands from across the table. "Hold dat thought, let me give Jehovah his due." She said a silent prayer over the food and said amen. "A'ight, baby, now go."

"I said I appreciate you."

Keisha smiled. "Thank you, baby, I appreciate you too. You always make sure that we have everything that we need. You ain't missed not one appointment, and ever since you found out I was pregnant, I can see a major change in you. So yeah, I appreciate you too."

Mudman looked her over. He knew he would kill a ma'fucka for her with no remorse. Keisha was his baby. He didn't know how things had progressed so swiftly, but they had. And it was safe to say that he was gone over her. "Keisha, I don't mean to sound soft and all of dat, but on everythang, shawty, I love the fuck out of you. I thank I been in love wit' you since way before you crossed over. Maybe cuz even doe I know you never really approved of me, you still took that time out to write me once a week. You visited me four times a month every month while I was up in Angola, you even took time out to grab Prentice's whip when I couldn't find you nobody to ride wit'. You was my rock. How da fuck could you hate me so much, and still go so hard for me?"

Keisha shrugged her shoulders. "You were still a human being, and don't nobody deserve what they was putting y'all through in Angola. Besides that, I never hated you. I always hated your ways, never you as a person. You're a good man, Rome, you know, underneath it all."

Mudman stood up. "Look, shawty, life is short as a bitch. Ma'fucka can be hurr today and gone tomorrow. I ain't got time to play dese games, mane, and you having my seed. Shawty, I love you, and just like I'm a real man in dem streets, I gotta be a real man to you as well. Fuck what the homeboys gon' say, it's 'bout you and my baby right now." He came around and knelt on one knee in front of her. "Keisha Kandace Miller, I need you to be my wife so we can do dis thang da right way. Will you be?" He opened the box and flashed the sparkling diamond ring.

Keisha's eyes were opened so wide that it was all Mudman could see in the darkness with the exceptions of what the candles shed light on. She sat looking down on him in disbelief. "Rome, are you absolutely sure, baby? There is so much that comes along with dis marriage thang. We got so much we gotta get in order before we take that route," Keisha said, getting ready to panic.

Now Mudman was feeling like an idiot. He slowly eased up from the floor and closed the Zales box. He pulled his chair from the table and sat back in it. "You know what, shawty? You right. I don't know what was wrong wit' me," he said, trying to save face. He felt like a pure idiot. Never again, he thought. Never again.

Keisha knew that she had offended him. She tried to rack her brain to come up with something to say that would ease his embarrassment. She reached across the table to touch his hand, but he pulled it back. She sat back defeated. "Baby, I didn't mean that I wouldn't marry you. I was just saying that we got a bit of work to do before we make that commitment. There is no doubt in my mind that I would rather be married before I become a mother. I feel like it's my right as a woman to be married first."

Mudman was too busy feeling like shit. "Let's just enjoy dis meal. Well talk about all dat other shit at another time."

Keisha could tell that he was offended, and she didn't know what to do, so instead of poking the bear and getting him more irritated than he already was, she just proceeded to eat her food, while Mudman felt like he needed to kill something to restore his manhood that had been lost.

Hood Rich

Chapter 17

Kayla woke up the next morning with her head pounding. Her stomach felt like it was turned upside down, and her mouth was drier than a desert. She yawned and squinted her eyes. It hurt just to have them open. She shielded them from the sun that was shining through the bedroom window and caught sight of Prentice just as he was injecting himself with the Sinaloa Tar. Prentice's eyes rolled into the back of his head. He felt like he was experiencing a million orgasms at once. Though he needed more and more of the Sinaloa to reach that feeling, when he reached it, he felt oh so good.

He opened his eyes and looked at her, for the first time seeing that she was awake. He pulled the rope from around his arm and injected the rest of the dope. He removed the syringe and hid it from her view. "Morning, baby girl."

Kayla ran her fingers through her hair. "Why do I feel like crap?" She groaned.

Prentice nodded for a second. He took his right hand and ran it across his face. "Cuz, baby, you just got a li'l taste of heaven, and now you back in hell." He laid his head back and smiled.

Kayla's head felt like she was being hit over it with a sledgehammer. She crawled across the bed. "What do I gotta do to get rid of this feeling?" Prentice had her up all night tooting Sinaloa. Her body, in just a short amount of time, had become addicted to it. Already she felt physically dependent.

Prentice licked his lips. He had something devilish on his mind. "You want me to help you ease that pain?" he asked.

Kayla felt like she was going to vomit. "Please, big bruh, I'll do anythang. I'll owe you."

Those were the words that Prentice wanted to hear. "A'ight, come here and sit on my lap."

Kayla rushed over to him. "I love you so much. Prentice. Damn, I always loved you."

Prentice laughed. He was a vet getting the next batch of dog food ready for Kayla. In a matter of five minutes. He had everything ready to go with the rope tied around her inner thigh. It felt hot and juicy in his hand, but it wasn't about sex in this moment. He had more devious plans on his mind.

"Why you finna put it down there?" she asked, watching him with her head tilted to the side.

Prentice rubbed the alcohol pad over the vein that popped up. As soon as it looked nice and plump, he pushed the needle inside of it. Kayla winced. "Hold on, shawty." She dug her nails into his shoulders. He pulled the rope from around her thigh and fed the poison into her system.

As she felt it going in, her eyes rolled to the back of her head. She came, moaning at the top of her lungs. She felt a sense of euphoria that the tooting had not been able to reach. "Lord, have mercy."

Prentice pulled the syringe out and slid from under her. He left her sitting in the chair nodding in and out. Drool came out of the corners of her mouth. "How you feeling, baby?" He watched her carefully.

She looked at him cock-eyed. It took all of her willpower to straighten her eyes. "I love you so much, Prentice," she slurred. "You always take such good care of me." She laid all the way back with her thighs wide open, her fat pussy on full display.

It looked so good to Prentice that he got to rubbing it. "I'ma always take care of you. You my baby girl, you hear me? You gon' be crazy 'bout me. You gon' ride for me, Kayla, like Keisha never did." He dropped down and stuck his head between her thighs, dead set on turning her out.

***

Five hours later, Kayla rolled a stolen Buick that Prentice had picked up. Prentice sat in the passenger's seat with a sawed off five shot automatic shotgun on his lap. He was hoping to catch one of the rival dope boys loafing. "Shawty, bend dis corner right hurr on Valley Park."

Kayla turned down the one way street. The first thing she saw were a group of dudes in the middle of the block. They were huddled up on one knee. She guessed that they were shooting dice. She was familiar with that sight in Baton Rouge. "Why we turning down here?" She could feel her sick already coming on. It wasn't bad, but there was a part of her brain that didn't want her body to become sober.

"'Cause, you 'bout to prove yo' love and loyalty to me, shawty. You steady hollering dat you love me shit. Well, we bout to see." He eyed the surroundings quickly. He saw that there were about five dudes in the middle of the block loafing, shooting dice. None of them looked like they were on point. He grabbed his ski mask from between his legs and threw it over his head. "Shawty, what I want you to do is pull over up thurr. I'm finna go out hurr and lay dese fuck niggas down. Dis da only way we gon' get some more of dat shit dat's making you feel so good. You do want some mo' of it, don't you?"

Kayla nodded, and looked around. "Yeah, but is dis the only way?"

"Hell yeah, it is." He nodded with his head to the spot that he wanted her to pull over in. "Now do like da fuck I say."

Kayla was unsure about what he was telling her to do, but at the same time, he had her hooked on the Sinaloa. She felt that if Prentice was telling her that the only way that she would be able to receive more of the drug is if she did what he told her to do, then she wasn't about to hesitate to follow his commands. She pulled over and ducked lower in her seat. Her heart was beating a mile a minute.

"When I give you the signal, you get yo' ass up out of dis car and pop that trunk, do you hear me?"

"Yes," Kayla said, looking around as best she could.

Prentice threw his hood over his head and slowly opened the door after making sure that he had his shotgun secure in his hand. He stepped on to the street. As soon as his foot hit the pavement, he rushed the crowd and upped the shotgun. "All you niggas lay it da fuck down!" he roared.

The dope boys took one look over their shoulders at him and took off running in every direction. Prentice got to bucking on his no mercy shit. Boo-wah! Chick-chick. Boo-wah! His second bullet zipped across the night and knocked a hole in the leg of one of the dope boys. He fell on his chest and tried to get up running. Prentice was on his ass. He ran over to him and kicked him in the back. The dope boy fell and scraped both of his knees on the concrete. Prentice waved his hand in the air at Kayla, giving her the signal to get up out of the car and pop the trunk.

She jumped up and out of the car and popped the trunk like Prentice had showed her with the screwdriver. She rushed back to the driver's seat and slid down. She was so scared that she felt like crying.

Prentice picked up the dope boy and threw him in the trunk. He slammed it closed with him hollering and beating against the back of it. "Get da fuck up out of here, shawty. Hurry up!"

Kayla stepped on the gas. The tires spun up smoke before thy scurried off in a zig zag fashion. "Holy shit, what we finna do wit' him?" she said in a panic. She could hear the dope boy going crazy in the trunk. He was hollering and kicking at the trunk.

"Just take Garfield all the way to the train station and jump on this tracks. When you see da swamp back dat way, I'ma tell you where to pull over at."

Kayla followed his commands. "Look, Prentice, after dis I gotta go home for a minute. I know my mama looking for me. She probably gon' go crazy when I walk into dat house."

"Shawty, shut yo' ass up. You finna finish dis shit right hurr wit me first, den we'll talk about you going home. Do you want some more of dat sweet shit or not?" Prentice snapped.

"Yeah, I do," she responded, jumping on the tracks and stepping on the gas. The car hopped up and down as it made its way down the path that the freight cars usually took. Kayla drove until she saw the swamp. As soon as it became visible, she looked over to Prentice.

He kept his silence. He was trying to figure out how to do what he was trying to do. "Shawty, you see that viaduct over date? Pull under that ma'fucka and throw dis bitch in park. You hear me?"

Kayla nodded. She was spooked. She didn't know what Prentice had on his mind, but she was starting to feel sick, not only from what was taking place, but because she was feening for the drug. Once again, she did exactly what Prentice instructed her to do.

Prentice hopped out of the car. The dope boy was still beating on the trunk like crazy. He sounded like he was freaking out. "Say, mane, let me out of dis ma'fucka. I don't know what is going on. Please just let me go."

Prentice beat on the top of the trunk with his fist. He had the shotgun in one hand, ready to aim and fire. "Say, nigga, shut yo' ass up. Shut yo' ass up or I'm finna blow through dis bitch," he threatened.

The dope boy calmed down. His leg was bleeding profusely. He felt like he was in the worst pain of his young life. The fact that he was rolling off of Mollie didn't help matters much. "A'ight, man. Please. Dis blood pouring out of me."

Prentice grabbed the zip ties from the glove box. "Look, I just wanna ask you some questions. You tell me what I wanna hurr, and you can go on 'bout yo' bidness, mane."

"Say, a'ight. Just let me up out of dis trunk, potna. I can't breathe!" the dope boy yelled, freaking out.

Prentice grabbed Kayla. "Come on, shawty, you finna zip tie dis nigga up while I hold this gun on him. All you gotta do is put his wrist in hurr and pull on dese. Can you do dat?"

Kayla clutched her stomach. She felt dizzy. "Prentice, I don't feel so good, big bruh. I think I'm finna be sick."

Prentice grabbed a handful of her hair and yanked her to him. "Did you hear what I asked you?"

"Yes," she whimpered.

He slammed the zip ties in her hand, then took the screwdriver out of his pocket and placed it into the keyhole of the old school Buick. "A'ight, nigga, I'm finna let yo' ass out, but just be still, or I'm rocking you. A'ight?"

"A'ight!" the dope boy yelled, growing irritated.

Prentice popped the lock and opened of up with the shotgun aimed at the dope boy. When it came all the way open, he saw the hustler curled into a ball. The entire inside of the trunk was coated in his blood. It smelled like copper and piss.

The dope boy held his arms in the air. He looked Spanish and Black. "Look, mane, I'll tell you anything you need to know. Just please don't take my life."

Prentice slung the shotgun and hit in dead in the mouth. "Shut the fuck up. Shawty, get yo' ass over hurr and tie dese wrists."

Kayla rushed to the trunk and followed his directives. The dope boy was bleeding at the mouth. He just wanted it all to be over. He felt dizzy and weak from the blood loss.

Once he was zip-tied, Prentice grabbed the other tie for Kayla and made her do his ankles as well. Then he pushed him as hard as he could and slipped behind Kayla. "A'ight, shawty, you wanna be my baby, right? You want me to spoil you like I be spoiling Keisha?" he asked and lied at the same time. Prentice had never spoiled Keisha, not even in the beginning of their relationship.

"Yes. I want you to help me get dis sick off of me," she said, one again clutching her stomach.

Prentice placed her finger around the trigger. "You see dis ma'fucka right hurr? You gon' aim dis big old gun at him and you gon' pull dis trigger. You do that, and you ain't never gotta worry about being sick again. I'ma take good care of you."

"Wait, what?" the dope boy heard this and began to panic. He tried to get up, but he was so woozy that he only stumbled, and fell back down. "You ain't ask me nothing. Ask me anything!" he hollered.

Prentice slipped from behind Kayla and made sure that the sawed off was on her shoulder the right way. "A'ight, baby, pop that bitch. Now! Pull da trigger."

Kayla felt her stomach turn over. She aimed it at the dope boy and closed her eyes just as he was coming to his feet. She pulled the trigger. Boo-wah!

The round exited and landed into his back. He felt the slug enter into him before it blew a massive hole out of his stomach. He looked down at it and saw that his guts were pouring out of him. He tried to holler, but no sound came out of his mouth, only blood, before he fell to the ground, lifeless.

Prentice jumped up and down, holding his phone. He'd recorded the entire event. "Hell yeah, shawty! Hell yeah! Dat's what I'm talking 'bout right thurr." He walked over to her and tongued her down. "You my muthafuckin' baby, you hear me?" He kissed on her some more before letting her go and putting his arm around her neck.

Kayla looked past him and to the dead dope boy. She couldn't believe her eyes. It seemed too surreal. She had taken someone's life. What did it mean? she wondered. She prayed that it didn't mean that she was going to hell as a pain shot through her stomach. "Oh, Prentice. I need you to help me get this feeling gone."

Prentice pulled a full syringe out of his inside jacket pocket. "I got you, and after dis, I'ma drop you off at home so you can get some rest. I'ma come get you in a day or so, 'cause I got something else dat I need you to take care of." He smiled sinisterly.

Chapter 18

Mudman sat in the passenger's seat guzzling a six ounce bottle of codeine and syrup. His eyes were low as a basement. He looked over at Figgady as he pushed the Dodge Durango around the South side of Baton Rouge. "So, you thank da best time for us to hit day ass is dis Thursday?" Mudman asked, taking another sip from his drink.

Figgady was fucked up off of Mollie and Lean. He was slumped on the driver's door with a Tech .9 on his lap. He already had a holster built into the door that held a Mossberg Pump. Baton Rouge had gotten deadly over the last few years, but it was normal to him. He knew how to change his killa mentality with the times. Chicago had put that murderous street shit in him before he was even twelve years old. He scanned the streets as he rolled down them, looking for any potential threats or targets. Even though he was up financially, he wasn't turning down no licks. That jack boy shit was a part of his soul.

"Mane, da way shawty saying how shit be, Thursdays is the best time to run up in dat bitch. Dem ma'fuckas be getting all the money and shit ready to go and cop more of dat Dominican Tar from dem boys out in the Dominican Republic. I guess they gotta send that cash to the islands, and on dat same day they get a drop off from them Cartel boys out West. While they are harvesting another shipment at their trap that gotta go all up and down the east coast. It's just crazy. Chela say they be running around like chickens wit' they heads cut off. So, if we can slip up in there and do what we gotta do, we can come away with a nice chunk of change, and product, but it has to be Thursday, or else we going on a blind mission."

"What she say dey security be like on dem days?" Mudman wanted to know. It already appeared to him that the Dominicans were dealing with two different forms of plugged Cartels, one out in the Dominican Republic, and of course, the Mexican Cartel out West. Mudman didn't know which one of the people were more deadly, but he knew for certain that neither crime syndicate was going to play about their money, or product. If they hit this lick, the drama was going to be tenfold. He was already imagining how it was all going to go down and putting together in his head how many men he thought they would need. No matter the number they started off with, he was going to see to it that they came home with near less than that. This was a life or death mission. Everything was on the table.

"Shawty say dey stay wit' dem choppas, mane. We gon' have to go in in straight bidness. Only reason I say Thursday is another good day to handle our bidness is because dey supposed to be having her cousin's baby shower dat day. Chela gon' make sure dat dey over dat way before they all disburse back to where day came from. We gon' hit dat bitch while da hoes is congregating. Dat's the softest time to do it."

Mudman nodded. He liked the sound of that. "So, it's gon' be a lot of her family dere den. Dat mean dem Dominican ma'fuckas will be more careful than to be bucking when dey got all dem chicks around, right?"

Figgady nodded. "Yeah, now you feeling me. I mean, we still gotta be ready to handle our bidness, 'cause dem niggas know they dealing with precious cargo dat don't belong to dem. Dem cartels don't give two fucks about dem hoes. Dey lose they shit, and dey coming fa dey heads, it's as simple as dat."

Mudman agreed. "A'ight den, we gon' roll out on Wednesday den. That way we can roll around Lawrence and Boston, you know, get a feel to what dat shit look like out dare. Where yo' shawty at right now?"

Figgady kept rolling. "She out dere wit' her people. I got my bitch taking pictures of everythang like she da feds. I need to know how every room in dat house look, and the face of da niggas we finna hit. Dis shit serious for me. The Ada B. Wells ain't raise no goofy." The Ada B. Wells was a heartless housing project out of Chicago, Illinois that Figgady was raised in.

Mudman laughed at that. "Yeah, a'ight, li'l homie. Make sho' you send me over dem flicks as you get 'em. Make sho' you hit up dat nigga Prentice too. We gon' make dis shit happen."

Figgady looked at him from the corners of his eyes. "Say Joe, dat shit between you and him squashed, ain't it?"

"What shit?"

Figgady sucked his teeth. "Come on now, big homie. I'm talking 'bout all dat fuck shit from da other day. Y'all ain't still beefing and fighting over no bitch, is you?"

Hearing Figgady refer to Keisha as a bitch made his blood boil quickly. Not only was she the mother of his child, but she was also the only female in the world that he loved outside of his own blood. He didn't want to expose his emotional hands, so he simply nodded. "Dat was just a misunderstanding. We good now."

"Yeah, I hope so. Dis move is life or death. Y'all gotta go in there with clear heads, or we gon' all die. Straight up." Figgady pulled up in front of the hotel that Mudman and Keisha were staying at.

Mudman got out of the whip and tucked his weapons. "We good, bruh. Just make sure I get dat footage. I'ma jam wit' you later."

Figgady threw up an L shape with his index finger and thumb. "Love, fool." He pulled away from the curb and looked into his rearview mirror. It was just as he suspected: the same Jeep Grand Cherokee had been following him for the last five minutes. He pulled his nose and nodded his head up and down. "Ma'fuckas wanna try me, huh? A'ight, let's do this then," he said out loud, cocking the Tech and placing it back on his lap.

***

Mudman stepped into the hotel room and closed the door behind him. The first thing he saw was Keisha sitting on the bed with her head down. She had the phone to her ear with a Kleenex in one hand. She looked up and saw him, then held up one finger."

Mudman locked the door and placed his guns all over the room in strategic places that he could get to them easily. He checked the mini refrigerator and pulled out a bag of White Castle burgers from the night before. After heating them up and dressing them, he sat down and began to eat.

Keisha hung up the phone and covered her face with her hands. "Fuck, fuck, fuck. I swear to God I'ma kill dat li'l girl," she promised.

Mudman kept eating. He really didn't want to get involved with Keisha's drama. As long as that stuff didn't have shit to do with him or the baby, he wanted to stay out of it. He grabbed his codeine and kept sipping. He turned on the television to SportsCenter.

Keisha stepped in front of the television and placed her hands on her hips. "Dang, ain't you gon' ask me what's wrong wit' me?"

He shook his head. "Nope. Clearly dat shit ain't got nothing to do wit' me. I ain't ate nothing all day. All I wanna do is enjoy my food."

Keisha screwed up her face and rolled her eyes. "Boy, whatever. You my muthafuckin' man, so you gon' listen to me. Turn dat damn TV off for a second."

Mudman bit into his sandwich and ignored her directives. "Dis ma'fucka ain't gotta be off for me to hurr you. Speak up and hurry up. The Laker game 'bout to come on, and you already know how I feel 'bout da King." Mudman didn't really like sports all that much, but when it came to LeBron James, he was tuned in.

Keisha smacked her lips and waved him off. "Ain't nobody thanking bout no damn king. My li'l sister been gone for two days, and when she finally came back home, my mama said she looked high and smelled like sex. Kayla been locked in her room ever since den. Mama said she been ignoring her."

Mudman looked at her like she was stupid. "And? Fuck dis gotta do wit' me?"

"She got a full scholarship to run track at LSU next year, and she could be fucking up her opportunity."

Mudman was no longer paying attention. "Keisha, I don't give no fuck. If you so concerned, why don't you go over dere and kick her ass? Otherwise, I don't know what the fuck to tell you," Mudman said, getting annoyed.

"Really, man?" She was heated.

He grabbed a pillow off of the bed and slung it at her with mild force. "Now get yo' ass from in front of the television screen. You making me miss some important highlights wit' my nigga."

"Uhhhh!" Keisha stomped her foot and moved out of the way. "I'm going over dere, I'll be back later."

Mudman turned up the volume on the television. "Later."

Ever since Keisha had botched his proposal, he had been treating her different. He still loved her, so it wasn't anything like that, but he just didn't know how to go there with her emotionally while the wound was still fresh. He would get it together soon - at least, he hoped.

***

Figgady glanced into his rearview mirror as he drove across Garfield. He made a right down the block and kept rolling. He glanced back into his mirrors, and sure enough, the Jeep did the same thing. They had been following him for another full ten minutes. He bent another corner and then hit a right and pulled into an alley. He stormed down it and made a left into a garage that was dead smack in the middle of it. As soon as he parked, he jumped out of his whip with the Tech .9, and two extra clips. He climbed out of the window of the garage and ran into the backyard that it was attached to. Then he hopped the fence, ran through that yard, and hopped a second fence. When he got into that yard, he rushed to the back of it toward the alley, just as the Jeep Cherokee came slowly down it, obviously searching for him. Figgady ducked down. He waited until the Jeep Cherokee got close enough before he jumped up and got to bucking. The Tech screamed in his hand, chopping up the side of the Jeep, shattering the windows on his side immediately.

The Jeep swerve, accelerated, and smashed into a light pole. The doors opened and three men jumped out with blue rags on their faces, busting at him with fully automatics. It sounded like the Fourth of July. Figgady could hear their bullets eating up the side of the garage where he was posted. He ran backward and all the way around to the next garage. He peered through the window of it and saw two of the men dropping clips from their guns and getting ready to reload. Figgady aimed and fired with the Tech spitting rapidly. He saw one of the men stand straight up and get filled with at least three bullets before he fell face first. This excited Figgady. He ducked back down, laughing crazily to himself. He pulled out the empty clip and smacked in another. This one had fifty shots, and he planned on using each one if he had to.

More shots chopped at his new location. He counted more than eighty, then it was suddenly quiet. He already knew what that meant. They must have been reloading. He ran out of the garage and into the alley on some kamikaze shit. It was kill or be killed, and he refused to wind up on the receiving end. He saw one man slamming a magazine into his weapon. He bum rushed him and slammed the barrel to his cheek, before pulling the trigger. His face vibrated on the Tech and was shredded.

The other shooter took off running down the alley. Figgady took off right behind him, busting. The shooter zigzagged and ran into somebody's yard. Figgady didn't know if he was still armed with bullets or if he was empty. He imagined himself following the path that the man had taken and running into a trap. He couldn't stand for that. Besides, the neighborhood that he was in was dangerous. The killas in the area had heard shooting. That meant that they were coming out to protect their homeland no matter what. This was Baton Rouge, Killa City. Figgady already knew what that meant, so he stopped in the alley and turned around. He broke back toward his truck. When he got to the man in the alley, he pulled his mask off and saw that he was Mexican. That was all that he needed to see. He knew that the Sinaloas were after them, and that their time was running out.

Keisha knocked on Kayla's door for the third time. "Kayla, open dis damn door, now!" she yelled.

Kayla nodded with her head in her lap. She wiped her mouth and looked at the door. She didn't feel like getting into it with Keisha. Her high was already dwindling down. She was trying to hold on to the last bits of it. "Keisha, what you want, mane? I'm in hurr trying to chill for a minute." She ran her hand over her face. Her body felt like it was floating. She scratched the injection site on her thigh.

Keisha was getting more and more vexed. She took a deep breath and tried to calm herself down. "Kayla, of you don't open dis damn door, I swear to God, when you finally do, I'ma kick yo' ass. Now open this damn door. Now." She said this through clenched teeth.

Kayla scooted to the edge of the bed and stood up. She moved to the door with her eyes closed, stepping on her shoe that was in the middle of the floor. She ran her hand over her face one more time before pulling the door open. "What, Keisha?"

Keisha busted in and bumped her out of the way. She looked around her messy room and noticed the smell of it. It smelled like she hadn't cleaned it in a few weeks. She saw that her schoolbooks, along with her clothes, were all over the floor. "What the fuck is going on up in hurr?"

Kayla ignored her and climbed into the bed. She got under the covers and pulled them over her head. "Leave me alone. I'm tired right now."

"You tired?" Keisha grabbed ahold of the blanket and ripped it from her. She slung it to the floor. "What the fuck is going on with you?"

Kayla opened her eyes. Her body continued to float. All she wanted to do was to enjoy the last part of her high. The more Keisha fucked with her, the faster she felt like it was dwindling. "Keisha, please, come back in a few hours. Damn, just leave me alone for a minute."

Keisha opened her eyes wide. She walked closer to the bed and looked her sixteen-year-old sister over. "Oh my God. Kayla, are you high?"

"What? Nall, Keisha, dang. Why don't you beat it? Please!" she screamed.

Keisha grabbed her by the face with one hand and squeezed it. "Girl, I'm finna beat yo' li'l ass if you high, on everythang."

Kayla jerked away from her and stood up. She grabbed a pair of pants and slid them up her gown. "I gotta get da fuck out of here. I need to just go." Her high was getting lower and lower, and already she felt her sick coming on. She didn't want to go through that all over again. She needed to find Prentice. He would know how to get her right. She loved him so much.

Keisha watched her closely. "What are you doing? Where are you finna go?"

"Out of dis house. I need to get far, far away from hurr." She pulled a blouse over her head.

Keisha ran and blocked the door. She had to piss, and she was trying her best to not focus in on that. But in the stage that she was in her pregnancy she found her bladder getting the best of her. "Kayla, I swear to sweet Jesus, that if you don't tell me what's going on, we about to tear this room up."

Kayla, stood there, looking at Keisha like she was crazy. "Keisha, I'm not about to fight you. I'm just going through something right now. Can't you just understand that?"

Keisha stepped forward. "Little sister, are you high?"

Kayla just wanted, Keisha to butt out. "Please, Keisha, dis ain't yo' bidness. Mind yours like I'm minding mine." She rolled her eyes and tried to go past Keisha.

Keisha, tired of the disrespect, swung and slapped the shit out of Kayla. Kayla fell to her knees, holding her face. "Now I don't know what the fuck is going on wit' you, but you gon' respect me. Is that understood?"

Kayla nodded her head. All that kept going through her mind was that she had to get out of that room. She slowly came to her feet. "I'm sorry, Keisha. I'm just going through something right now."

"Girl, is it drugs?" Keisha inquired, stepping closer to her sister.

Kayla nodded. "Yeah." She clutched her stomach.

Keisha held her mouth. "Damn, sis, what kind?"

Tears fell from Kayla's eyes. "Heroin, and it got me fucked up too, but I'ma be okay." She didn't know why she'd told Keisha that. She guessed because she'd never kept a secret from her older sister before, so it had just come out so naturally. But now that she'd said it, she knew that she'd said too much.

"Heroin? What da fuck is wrong wit' you? Are you out of your fuckin' mind?" she screamed.

Kayla knew that she'd made the wrong decision in telling her right then. "I'm out of here."

Keisha grew furious. "You li'l bitch, no you ain't." She ran at Kayla.

Kayla stood her ground. She waited until Keisha got close before she jumped on the bed and ran around her. She got to the door first and opened it. She dashed into the hallway and out of the house. "I ain't coming back to dis ma'fucka. Prentice gon' take care of me!" she screamed.

As soon as Keisha heard the name Prentice, she grew sick. She got to putting the pieces of the puzzle together. It didn't take her long before she had basically put together the entire picture. Prentice had purposely turned her sister out to get back at her. She couldn't believe how low he had sunk, by then again, of course she could. She sank to her knees and bawled her eyes out.

***

An hour later, Prentice scooped Kayla up in his black Benz truck. She jumped inside and closed the door. Tears ran down her eyes. "I hate her, I swear to God I do," Kayla cried, feeling her stomach turn over. She had a migraine that felt like it was threatening to blind her.

Prentice pulled away from the curb. "Who are you talking about?"

"Keisha. She just tried to lock me into my room. I know my mama called her over to deal with me. I don't know why they think I'm somebody's child?"

Price rolled for a second in silence. "You tell her where you was going?"

"Nope, I would never do that," she whimpered, wiping her eyes.

He was silent again. His phone vibrated in his lap. He looked at the face and saw that it was the fiftieth message from Keisha. She was blaming him for Kayla's drug use and saying that if Kayla didn't come home that she was going to call the police on him, and all types of other shit. He was so mad that he didn't know what to do. "You sho' you ain't tell yo' sister dat you was going wit' me?"

"Positive, I would never do dat." She sniffled and wiped her nose. "Do you believe me?"

Prentice shook his head. "Nall, bitch, I don't, but dat's neither here nor there. What is yo' end game hurr?"

She shrugged her shoulders. "I don't know. I thought I was gon' come and live wit' you. You would take me in, right?"

Prentice nodded. "You know that."

Kayla smiled. "I figured you would." She sat back in her seat and got comfortable, but the task was impossible. Her stomach hurt, and now she was feeling like she had to shit. "Prentice, can you get me right, baby? Please?"

Prentice nodded. He pulled a hot shot out of his coat pocket. A hot shot was a syringe hooked up with so much dope that it could possibly bust a person's heart. Prentice had hooked up a batch of Sinaloa that was sure to do just that to Kayla. He didn't give a fuck about her. His sole mission in fucking with her was to hurt Keisha in the worst way possible. "Baby, I got somethin for you dat's gon' make you feel real good, trust me." Prentice stopped briefly at the stop sign at the corner of Maple Street, and then pulled off into traffic

"Oh, I do, I do Prentice. You always take care of me. If it wasn't for you, I already know I would be messed up out here." She was so happy about the news that she didn't know what to do.

Prentice jumped on the highway and rolled for fifteen minutes until he got to the north side across East Town, located past 22nd Street. He pulled under a viaduct and threw the truck in park. East Town was known for heroin addicts. "Come on back here, and let's handle dis bidness."

Kayla pulled her seat belt off of her and beat him to the back of the truck. "Thank you so much, Prentice. I swear I love you so much. I would do anything for you. I promise I would." She pulled down her pants and exposed her thigh.

"I can't find a vein in this dark. You gon' have to do it for me."

Prentice shook his head. "Nall, Shawty, we gon' get you a real good one right hurr in this inner forearm." He took an alcohol pad and rubbed it all over the area.

Kayla felt like she was about to hyperventilate. "Please, let's go. Please, Prentice."

"Oh, before we do that, I'ma need you to fuck wit' Keisha's head a li'l bit. I don't need her to know dat you wit' me. I need you to fool her, and act like you disappearing off dis earth all together. Dat way dey don't come looking for you, and we can be happy together from here on out. You feel me?"

Kayla got the shivers. The smell of the alcohol pad was driving her insane. That scent was usually followed by the happiness of the Sinaloa. "Prentice, please, I'll do anything. Let's just hurry this up. Please."

Prentice smiled and grabbed a burner phone. "Look, you gon' Facetime Keisha and tell her that you can't take it no more. That you tired of living, and dat they put too much pressure on you for yo' school shit. Tell her you taking yo life, that it's her fault, and end the video. You got that?"

Kayla nodded. "Yes."

"A'ight, come on." Prentice grabbed her by the wrist and made her stand against the brick wall. She held the phone in front of her and did exactly what he told her to do. He could hear Keisha trying to reason with her. Kayla screamed into the phone and disconnected the call. She staggered over and handed the phone to Prentice.

Prentice took it and gave her the syringe. "Here you go, boo, enjoy."

Kayla took the syringe and squared down Indian Style. She grabbed the rope that Prentice tossed to her and stuck the needle into her arm. When it was set, she pulled it off, and injected the hot shot into her system. She felt the heat of it shoot up her vein. It felt like fire. The path was quick. She tried to stand up, but only managed to get halfway before, it attacked her heart and the pressure caused it to bust right away. She took a deep breath and fell face first to the ground, shaking, and convulsing, and then she was dead.

Prentice stood over her with an evil sneer on his face. He poked at her with his shoe, confirming that she was out for the count. He took the syringe out of her arm, along with the rope from the ground and jumped back into his truck, pulling away. Kayla's death made him only feel a little better. He had a whole lot more to do before the black hole that Keisha had created could be closed up in in his heart.

***

Keisha got the call at one on the morning. She rushed over to meet her mother Kimmie at the site where they were saying that they had just found her sister. When she got there, her mother was already breaking down and being held up by her oldest sister, Karmen. Keisha rushed over to them. The area was flooded with the police and ambulances. Kayla had a white sheet draped over her body. Keisha stopped midway to her family and looked out at the scene. She couldn't believe it.

Kimmie ran over to Kayla's body, screaming at the top of her lungs. She grabbed the sheet and pulled it off. Kayla lay with her eyes wide open. This made Kimmie scream even louder. Keisha fell to the ground with her mother hugging her. The only person on her mind was Prentice. Deep in her heart, she knew that he was responsible.

Chapter 20

It was nine o'clock at night on a breezy night. Mudman circled the block around the Dominican's trap house. He saw that there was one van parked in front of it. He imagined that the van belonged to the men inside that were set to make the moves all up and down the east coast. He looked over at the complex, and then to Prentice, who sat in the passenger's seat sipping on a bottle of water that was spiked with Mollie. "What you thanking, homeboy?"

"I say we trust li'l homie. He say his bitch in durr wit' a few other hoes. If dat's the case, then dem niggas gon' be less likely to pop dem guns. We gotta get in and get out, it's as simple as dat."

Figgady shook his head. "You damn right we gotta do dat. My shawty in durr right now doing everythang she supposed to be doing. She gon' have on a yellow and white Hermes dress. Y'all make sure dat when we run in dis bitch dat don't nobody make a mistake and pop her. She gon' be branging some garbage out in ten minutes. I'ma snatch her up and take her back in dere. Dat's when you niggas move and go in dat bitch. My li'l crew gon' run in first wit' choppas, followed by you. The money bags gon' be in the first room to da left, along with the weight. She say the choppas piled up in green crates in the room next to the bathroom. It's five niggas inside. I don't know how many are armed, but dey all leaning, and gone off of dat shit, so da odds are in our favor. Everybody ready to go?" he asked, looking around.

In addition to Prentice and Mudman, there were four other men inside of the truck. Mudman considered the men along for the ride to be his aces. All of them had earned his respect, and when it all came down to it, he wanted to make

171

sure that they had a firm understanding before they took part in such a dangerous mission. "Look, mane, dis is life-altering money. We need to go in hurr and get dis shit done right. Da faster we get in, da faster we can be back on the road to Baton Rouge, y'all feel me? Everybody got dem new vests on, right?"

Each man nodded their heads - all except for Prentice. He wasn't feeling Mudman. He felt like he always had to have the last word. In his opinion, Mudman was a bitch, and he couldn't wait until they got this big bag so he could finally smoke his ass. Then he would finish off Keisha.

Figgady shook up with Mudman. "Look, I'm putting you niggas up on dis lick because I want everybody to eat off of the same plate with the same portions. Ain't nobody sitting hurr better den da next man in dis crew, you feel dat?"

They all kept silent. Neither Mudman nor Prentice agreed with that statement. They just wanted to get on with the mission. They didn't need a pep talk like most niggas.

"Look, let's get dis shit on the road. Time is mutha-fuckin' money. Me and Mudman gon take the back door, Figgady, you and him right hurr take the front, since dat's where Chela coming out of, and the rest of the men gon' flood those entrance ways. All the product goes to dis hurr van right hurr. When we get away, we drive those ten blocks down and split it up into three cars. Everybody understand? A'ight, let's get it."

***

Figgady and Poo loafed on the side of the house directly across from the hit spot. He had just received a text from Chela saying that she was going to be making her way outside. He looked through his binoculars and saw the front door opening. Sure enough, there was his baby mother. She walked on the side of her cousin. She looked like she needed to be held up. When they got all the way outside of the door, Chela rushed to the grass and threw up.

Figgady dropped the binoculars. "A'ight, niggas, it's a go. Let's go handle dis shit."

He jumped up and hunched down. He ran across the street with the Tech .9 in his hand. He was followed by three other men. When he got by Chela, he waved the other men past him. They rushed toward the house. Chela's cousin got ready to scream. Figgady cocked back and punched her as hard as he could directly in the mouth, knocking her out cold. "Take yo' ass across the street and wait for me."

She nodded and ran across the street, feeling sick to her stomach for real. She watched from a distance as Figgady disappeared inside of the trap house. She prayed that nobody got killed, but then again, she knew better.

Mudman waited until the gunfire started before he raised his foot, and then he slammed it against the door with all of his might. It splintered. Then he crashed into it with his shoulder and busted through the door. He stumbled at first but caught his balance. The back door led into a hallway. The inside of the house had every light on. A bunch of females started to scream and run, trying to get out of the way. Prentice hurried past him and into the living room, where two Dominicans were on their knees bucking at Figgady and his shooters. Prentice aimed and got ready to fire, but before he could, Mudman rushed them and gave them dome shots in the back of the heads, knocking their brains out the front of their faces. He stepped past them and disappeared.

Prentice got irritated. He felt like Mudman had stolen his kill from him, much like he did everything else. He couldn't wait to slump his ass when the time was right, he kept reminding himself. When the time was right. He ran off to get himself immersed in the gun battle. Before he could got halfway down the hallway, a door opened. He didn't think. He knelt down and finger-fucked his trigger, knocking the head off of one of Chela's female cousins. He mugged her body for a second and kept running.

Figgady caught two to the vest and flew into the wall. It felt like he'd been kicked in the chest by a bull. He slid to the floor, struggling to breathe. Shots continued to come him way. He busted his Tech at the Dominican that had flipped the table for cover. The Dominican sprayed with his Draco, and Figgady's young hitta fell in front of him with four bullets in for forehead.

Figgady scooted back on the floor, busting.

Mudman ran full speed out of the hallway, slammed his Mach .90 to the Dominican's ear, and pulled the trigger. His noodles sprayed the curtains and painted them a burgundy red. Then he laid flat out on his stomach. Mudman caught two to the back and landed on top of the man that he had just killed. Another Dominican rushed over and aimed, ready to punch his lights out. Prentice caught sight and fired, running toward the man, hitting him in the neck three times. The man fell beside Mudman. He stood over him and popped him three more times. He and Mudman locked eyes, before he ran off. Prentice wasn't preventing the man from killing Mudman because he wanted to save his cousin. No, that wasn't the case. No, he simply wanted to be the one that killed his cousin. He wasn't about to allow nobody to take that away from him.

More shooting ensued. Then the rest of their cartel rushed in on bidness, slaying everything moving. When it was all said and done, Mudman, Prentice, and Figgady were forced to grab all of their spoils of war while stepping over bodies and slipping on blood. The van pulled to the back of the house and bag after bag was tossed into it, followed by gun after gun. They stripped the house to the bone and only managed to leave behind four members of their cartel. For Mudman, this was a good lick.

Hood Rich

Chapter 21

It was two days later, and Keisha was still messed up about what had taken place with Kayla. She hadn't gotten one wink of sleep or eaten one morsel of food. Mudman was worried about her. He felt that all of her depression was bad for their baby. The last thing he wanted to happen at this juncture was for Keisha to have a miscarriage due to stress. He entered into the dark living room that she was sitting in and sat on the couch next to her. He took her hands inside of his and moved her curls out of her face. He kissed her cheek.

"Baby, please, tell me what I can do to take you out of dis slump. Dis shit can't be good for da baby."

Keisha wiped her tears and looked over to him. She could only make out most of his face by the moonlight coming through the windows. "I know Prentice did dis shit, Rome. He got my sister strung out on dat shit, and her body couldn't handle it. He did all dat just to get back at me. It's all my fault," she cried. "She was so precious."

Mudman pulled her into his embrace. He was skeptical. He couldn't see Prentice being that fuckin' petty. I mean, he knew that his cousin was grimy, but to go above and beyond to do all of that just seemed a little farfetched. He gave him more player points than that. "Shawty, how you know that yo' li'l sister ain't fall in wit' da wrong crowd at school or something? She already said she felt like it was too much pressure on her at school. Maybe the drugs was a coping mechanism, at least until she couldn't take dat shit no more."

Keisha turned to look at him. "So, what, you taking his side now?" she asked, standing up. She was mad at the world, and Mudman was the closest person she could take it out on.

Mudman sighed. "Shawty, you tripping, it ain't nothing like dat."

"Den why you ain't out dere fanning his ass down? I'm telling you he did this, and you just been sitting hurr the last couple days like it don't even matter." She fell to her knees and broke down crying. "Why would he do that to my sister, mane? She was only sixteen years old. She was my best friend, and she had her whole life ahead of her. Ohhh, I hate him so much. I hate his fuckin' guts. It's all my fault." She rocked back and forth on her knees. "It's all my fault."

Mudman hopped up and sent Prentice a text saying that he needed him to meet him at the house. He wanted to get to the bottom of it all once and for all.

***

Twenty minutes later, Prentice stood in the basement of Mudman's trap while Keisha sat on the couch with her eyes red as fireballs. She had bags under them, and she felt weaker than a person with pneumonia. Every time she thought about Kayla, it caused her to break down. She prayed that she was living inside of a bad dream.

"Why da fuck am I hurr, mane?"

"Keisha wanna ask you a question, Dat's it. Dat's all," Mudman said looking over his shoulder.

"Man, I ain't got nothing to say to dat rotten-ass bitch. Far as I'm concerned, that bitch dead to me," he snapped, looking past Mudman's shoulder.

Mudman felt his temper warming up. "Say, potna, we ain't hurr for all dat shit dat. Nigga, she got a simple-ass question, and we can be on with dis shit. Me and shawty finna stab out of Baton Rouge, and before we go, she just wanna ask you a question."

Prentice kept mugging Keisha. He could tell that she was pregnant, and it was making him become irate. "What da fuck she wanna ask me?"

Keisha turned to them. "Did you get my sister hooked on dat shit that took her life?" She jumped up and took two steps toward them.

Prentice smiled. "Bitch got way better pussy den you do. Knew how to ride dis ma'fucka and all dat. Damn shame she couldn't handle that dope doe. Shit might have been too pure. Oops." He covered his mouth with one hand before taking it away and laughing. "How dat make your trifling ass feel?"

"Damn." Mudman lowered his head. He couldn't believe his ears.

"I knew you did it. I knew you killed my sister!" Keisha rushed to the couch and slid her hand under it. She came up with Mudman's .40 Glock. She already had it cocked. She raised it and aimed at Prentice.

Prentice came from under his shirt with two .9s. He cocked back the hammers and got to shooting to kill. It was the moment he had been praying for...

To Be Continued...
Cartel Killaz 2
Coming Soon

Submission Guideline

Submit the first three chapters of your completed manuscript to ldpsubmissions@gmail.com, subject line: Your book's title. The manuscript must be in a .doc file and sent as an attachment. Document should be in Times New Roman, double spaced and in size 12 font. Also, provide your synopsis and full contact information. If sending multiple submissions, they must each be in a separate email.

Have a story but no way to send it electronically? You can still submit to LDP/Ca$h Presents. Send in the first three chapters, written or typed, of your completed manuscript to:

LDP: Submissions Dept
Po Box 870494
Mesquite, Tx 75187

DO NOT send original manuscript. Must be a duplicate.

Provide your synopsis and a cover letter containing your full contact information.

Thanks for considering LDP and Ca$h Presents.

Coming Soon from Lock Down Publications/Ca$h Presents

BOW DOWN TO MY GANGSTA

By **Ca$h**

TORN BETWEEN TWO

By **Coffee**

BLOOD STAINS OF A SHOTTA **III**

By **Jamaica**

STEADY MOBBIN **III**

By **Marcellus Allen**

RENEGADE BOYS IV

By Meesha

BLOOD OF A BOSS **VI**

SHADOWS OF THE GAME II

By **Askari**

LOYAL TO THE GAME **IV**

LIFE OF SIN **III**

By **T.J. & Jelissa**

A DOPEBOY'S PRAYER **II**

By **Eddie "Wolf" Lee**

IF LOVING YOU IS WRONG... **III**

By **Jelissa**

TRUE SAVAGE **VII**

By **Chris Green**

BLAST FOR ME **III**

DUFFLE BAG CARTEL **IV**

HEARTLESS GOON **II**

By **Ghost**

A HUSTLER'S DECEIT III

KILL ZONE **II**

BAE BELONGS TO ME III

SOUL OF A MONSTER III

By **Aryanna**

THE COST OF LOYALTY **III**

By **Kweli**

A GANGSTER'S SYN III

THE SAVAGE LIFE II

By **J-Blunt**

KING OF NEW YORK V

RISE TO POWER III

COKE KINGS IV

BORN HEARTLESS II

By **T.J. Edwards**

GORILLAZ IN THE BAY IV

De'Kari

THE STREETS ARE CALLING II

Duquie Wilson

KINGPIN KILLAZ IV

STREET KINGS III

PAID IN BLOOD III

CARTEL KILLAZ II

Hood Rich

SINS OF A HUSTLA II

ASAD

TRIGGADALE III

Elijah R. Freeman

KINGZ OF THE GAME IV

Playa Ray

SLAUGHTER GANG IV

RUTHLESS HEART

By Willie Slaughter

THE HEART OF A SAVAGE II

By Jibril Williams

FUK SHYT II

By Blakk Diamond

THE DOPEMAN'S BODYGAURD II

By Tranay Adams

TRAP GOD II

By Troublesome

YAYO II

By S. Allen

GHOST MOB

Stilloan Robinson

KINGPIN DREAMS

By Paper Boi Rari

CREAM

By Yolanda Moore

Available Now
RESTRAINING ORDER **I & II**
By **CA$H & Coffee**
LOVE KNOWS NO BOUNDARIES **I II & III**
By **Coffee**
RAISED AS A GOON I, II, III & IV
BRED BY THE SLUMS I, II, III
BLAST FOR ME I & II
ROTTEN TO THE CORE I II III
A BRONX TALE I, II, III
DUFFEL BAG CARTEL I II III
HEARTLESS GOON
A SAVAGE DOPEBOY
HEARTLESS GOON
By **Ghost**
LAY IT DOWN **I & II**
LAST OF A DYING BREED
BLOOD STAINS OF A SHOTTA I & II
By **Jamaica**
LOYAL TO THE GAME
LOYAL TO THE GAME II
LOYAL TO THE GAME III
LIFE OF SIN I, II
By **TJ & Jelissa**
BLOODY COMMAS I & II
SKI MASK CARTEL I II & III
KING OF NEW YORK I II,III IV

RISE TO POWER I II
COKE KINGS I II III
BORN HEARTLESS
By **T.J. Edwards**
IF LOVING HIM IS WRONG…I & II
LOVE ME EVEN WHEN IT HURTS I II III
By **Jelissa**
WHEN THE STREETS CLAP BACK I & II III
By **Jibril Williams**
A DISTINGUISHED THUG STOLE MY HEART I II & III
LOVE SHOULDN'T HURT I II III IV
RENEGADE BOYS I II III
By **Meesha**
A GANGSTER'S CODE I &, II III
A GANGSTER'S SYN I II
THE SAVAGE LIFE
By J-Blunt
PUSH IT TO THE LIMIT
By **Bre' Hayes**
BLOOD OF A BOSS **I, II, III, IV, V**
SHADOWS OF THE GAME
By **Askari**
THE STREETS BLEED MURDER **I, II & III**
THE HEART OF A GANGSTA I II& III
By **Jerry Jackson**
CUM FOR ME
CUM FOR ME 2

185

Hood Rich

CUM FOR ME 3

CUM FOR ME 4

CUM FOR ME 5

An **LDP Erotica Collaboration**

BRIDE OF A HUSTLA **I II & II**

THE FETTI GIRLS **I, II& III**

CORRUPTED BY A GANGSTA I, II III, IV

BLINDED BY HIS LOVE

By **Destiny Skai**

WHEN A GOOD GIRL GOES BAD

By **Adrienne**

THE COST OF LOYALTY I II

By Kweli

A GANGSTER'S REVENGE **I II III & IV**

THE BOSS MAN'S DAUGHTERS

THE BOSS MAN'S DAUGHTERS II

THE BOSSMAN'S DAUGHTERS III

THE BOSSMAN'S DAUGHTERS IV

THE BOSS MAN'S DAUGHTERS **V**

A SAVAGE LOVE **I & II**

BAE BELONGS TO ME I II

A HUSTLER'S DECEIT I, II, III

WHAT BAD BITCHES DO I, II, III

SOUL OF A MONSTER I II

KILL ZONE

By **Aryanna**

A KINGPIN'S AMBITON

A KINGPIN'S AMBITION **II**

I MURDER FOR THE DOUGH

By **Ambitious**

TRUE SAVAGE

TRUE SAVAGE II

TRUE SAVAGE **III**

TRUE SAVAGE **IV**

TRUE SAVAGE **V**

TRUE SAVAGE **VI**

By **Chris Green**

A DOPEBOY'S PRAYER

By **Eddie "Wolf" Lee**

THE KING CARTEL **I, II & III**

By **Frank Gresham**

THESE NIGGAS AIN'T LOYAL **I, II & III**

By **Nikki Tee**

GANGSTA SHYT **I II &III**

By **CATO**

THE ULTIMATE BETRAYAL

By **Phoenix**

BOSS'N UP **I , II & III**

By **Royal Nicole**

I LOVE YOU TO DEATH

By Destiny J

I RIDE FOR MY HITTA

I STILL RIDE FOR MY HITTA

By **Misty Holt**

LOVE & CHASIN' PAPER

By **Qay Crockett**

TO DIE IN VAIN

SINS OF A HUSTLA

By **ASAD**

BROOKLYN HUSTLAZ

By **Boogsy Morina**

BROOKLYN ON LOCK I & II

By **Sonovia**

GANGSTA CITY

By **Teddy Duke**

A DRUG KING AND HIS DIAMOND I & II III

A DOPEMAN'S RICHES

HER MAN, MINE'S TOO I, II

CASH MONEY HO'S

By Nicole Goosby

TRAPHOUSE KING **I II & III**

KINGPIN KILLAZ I II III

STREET KINGS I II

PAID IN BLOOD **I II**

CARTEL KILLAZ

By **Hood Rich**

LIPSTICK KILLAH **I, II, III**

CRIME OF PASSION I & II

By **Mimi**

STEADY MOBBN' **I, II, III**

By **Marcellus Allen**

WHO SHOT YA **I, II, III**

Renta

GORILLAZ IN THE BAY **I II III**

DE'KARI

TRIGGADALE I II

Elijah R. Freeman

GOD BLESS THE TRAPPERS I, II, III

THESE SCANDALOUS STREETS I, II, III

FEAR MY GANGSTA I, II, III

THESE STREETS DON'T LOVE NOBODY I, II

BURY ME A G I, II, III, IV, V

A GANGSTA'S EMPIRE I, II, III, IV

THE DOPEMAN'S BODYGAURD

Tranay Adams

THE STREETS ARE CALLING

Duquie Wilson

MARRIED TO A BOSS… I II III

By Destiny Skai & Chris Green

KINGZ OF THE GAME I II III

Playa Ray

SLAUGHTER GANG I II III

By Willie Slaughter

THE HEART OF A SAVAGE

By Jibril Williams

FUK SHYT

By Blakk Diamond

DON'T F#CK WITH MY HEART I II

By Linnea

ADDICTED TO THE DRAMA I II III

By Jamila

YAYO

By S. Allen

TRAP GOD

By Troublesome

BOOKS BY LDP'S CEO, CA$H

TRUST IN NO MAN

TRUST IN NO MAN 2

TRUST IN NO MAN 3

BONDED BY BLOOD

SHORTY GOT A THUG

THUGS CRY

THUGS CRY 2

THUGS CRY 3

TRUST NO BITCH

TRUST NO BITCH 2

TRUST NO BITCH 3

TIL MY CASKET DROPS

RESTRAINING ORDER

RESTRAINING ORDER 2

IN LOVE WITH A CONVICT

Coming Soon

BONDED BY BLOOD 2

BOW DOWN TO MY GANGSTA

Hood Rich

CPSIA information can be obtained
at www.ICGtesting.com
Printed in the USA
LVHW041539171219
640804LV00012B/1041/P